THE MODOC KID

Oregon, 1873. Michael Barncho is charged with the murder of an American general. He and his fellow conspirators face a military tribunal at Fort Klamath. The Nation is crying out for revenge. Found guilty, the death sentence is a formality. Chained together, the condemned men are led to the gallows, but Barncho survives in the most bizarre fashion. Dubbed 'The Modoc Kid' he is hunted, hated and feared, as Fate leads him along a trail of ordeal and murder that will end with a life-sentence in the fog-bound hell-hole called Alcatraz, the notorious prison in San Francisco Harbour.

THE MODOC KID

THE MODOC KID

by

Mark Bannerman

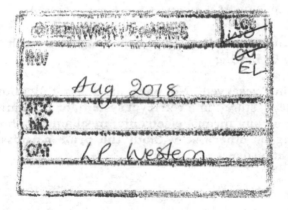

Dales Large Print Books
Long Preston, North Yorkshire,
BD23 4ND, England.

British Library Cataloguing in Publication Data.

Bannerman, Mark
    The Modoc kid.

    A catalogue record of this book is
    available from the British Library

    ISBN   978-1-84262-575-0 pbk

First published in Great Britain in 2006 by Pipers' Ash Ltd.

Copyright © Anthony Lewing 2006

Cover illustration © Gordon Crabb by arrangement with
Alison Eldred

The moral right of the author has been asserted

Published in Large Print 2007 by arrangement with
Anthony C. Lewing

Dales Large Print is an imprint of Library Magna Books Ltd.

Printed and bound in Great Britain by
T.J. (International) Ltd., Cornwall, PL28 8RW

This Book is Dedicated to
My Good Friend
JOHN GREASLEY

FORWARD

This narrative is not a story of the Indian wars but an account of one man's struggle for survival.

By the 1860's the Modoc Indian tribe whose lands straddled the Oregon and California borders had been decimated by white encroachment. Under their chieftain, Old Schonchin, the Modocs eventually agreed to move to the Yainax reservation near the Sprague River. They were obliged to share this with their age-old adversaries the Klamath Indians. The Modocs were given the poorest section, the Klamaths abused Modoc women, prevented the harvesting of crops, destroyed fences and commandeered the best supplies. The reservation authorities did nothing to alleviate the situation and old Schonchin was too senile to intervene. But the sub-chiefs Captain Jack and Hooker Jim were not so tolerant and led their followers off the reservation and set up villages thirty miles away along the Lost River. Here, there were plenty of camus bulbs, wocus roots and edible water-lily seeds, game abounded and the river was rich with trout, perch and suckers.

For five years the Modocs roamed freely. But in 1872, the government decided these Indians must return to the reservation and an army column was dispatched to force them back. However the Modocs resisted. Shots were exchanged and Indian wickiups torched. Captain Jack and his followers, including families, crossed Tule Lake by canoe to the Lava Beds. Here ancient volcanic eruption had sprayed hot lava over an area of about fifty square miles. This terrain comprised of countless ridges. Within these, in a congealed mass of lava, the Modocs established their Stronghold and prepared to repel attack. Meanwhile Hooker Jim and his band rampaged, attacked homesteads and killed fourteen male settlers. Afterwards they joined Captain Jack in the Stronghold.

Whilst Jack had not committed violence himself, he felt obligated to provide sanctuary for Hooker Jim. All the renegade Modocs were thus viewed collectively as hostiles.

The army launched an onslaught on these renegades but the task was tougher than anticipated. The bluecoats were met by deadly fire, felling many of them onto the razor-sharp rocks. The Stronghold proved a perfect defensive position. Finally the soldiers retreated, discarding equipment which the Indians collected for their own use.

In desperation, General Canby, Commander of the Department of Columbia, arranged to meet Captain Jack half-way between the military and Indian lines to discuss peace terms. But the Modocs suspected treachery. Hooker Jim, the shaman Curley Headed Doctor and their supporters taunted Jack, saying that he lacked the courage to fight. They persuaded him to murder General Canby in the belief that the bluecoats would then leave the Modocs alone. Jack knew that unless he complied with this request he would be deposed as chief. Therefore, reluctantly, he agreed the plan.

On Good Friday 1873, the Indian party met General Canby and his peace commissioners as arranged. After unsuccessful talking, tempers boiled over. Captain Jack murdered the general. The surviving commissioners fled to the army camp, while the Indians returned to their Stronghold.

The general's killing sparked consternation throughout the nation. However the Indians might have remained in the Stronghold had they not argued amongst themselves. Eventually the entire band, warriors and families, left the Stronghold through a concealed dip in the ground, passing close to the military lines, thereafter scattering into separate groups. Tracking them across the cruel terrain was difficult.

Hooker Jim eventually surrendered to the army and agreed to reveal Captain Jack's location in exchange for his own immunity. His offer was accepted and he led soldiers to Jack's concealed camp at Willow Creek.

Jack, a handful of warriors, fifteen squaws and seven children gave themselves up. Reassurance was given that they would not face retribution. However this proved false. Jack and five of his followers were placed on trial at Fort Klamath and jointly found guilty of murdering General Canby. All six were sentenced to death. One of them was called Barncho.

His story has haunted me. Now I believe it cries out to be told.

M.B.

CHAPTER ONE

People will ask what it is like to face death within a half-hour. I will tell how I try to shut myself away from my present and think of the old days. I live again our wonderful freedom in the land we call Mawatoc, where vast forests of ponderosa pine clothe the land; and elsewhere there are alkali flats scattered with sagebrush and juniper. To the east, antelope and bighorn sheep graze the lava fields. There are tule-fringed lakes and marshland where ducks, geese, pelicans and gulls abound. In summer the blue skies are cruised by hawks and owls. Overlooking everything is Mount Shasta, draped in violet shadows, white topped and haunted by sacred spirits.

Of course everything changed when, just after surrendering to the bluecoats at Willow Creek, we realized that we had been tricked, that promises of the Grandfather's mercy were lies. We had been sickened by the constant hounding; our families, many old and blind, were exhausted.

But it was better than what we now face.

We still pray for mercy to Kumookumts, the greatest of all spirits who gave birth to an infant from his knee. We pray that he will save us, but I believe he is looking away.

It is twelve weeks since the white man's judge pronounced that we would be hanged at such time and place as the authorities directed.

The morning sunlight streams through our small grating. The six of us are confined in the fort's guardhouse, in a tiny cell which smells of the latrine. We have become oblivious to the stench. Flies buzz in the stifling atmosphere. We sit with our backs against the wall, our chins on our drawn-up knees; weeks of chafing iron have rendered our ankles raw. We do not speak. From beyond the parade ground come sounds of the gathering crowd. Settlers have poured in from afar to watch the executions, and some Modocs and Klamaths have come from the agency at Yainax. We can hear the excited murmur of their voices. Everybody will be asking the same question. Will the condemned, the so-called ring-leaders, die with courage? Or will they perish as snivelling cowards?

One thing we all know: it is a Modoc belief that when a man dies at a rope's-end instead of being cremated, his spirit will be suffocated and prevented from reaching the after-life. The Sunday Doctor tried to persuade us otherwise, saying that we have nothing to fear because the next world is paradise. Why would he not come with us if it was so wonderful?

Fort Klamath is situated where the grass provides ample forage for army horses in the Wood River Valley. On the west and north are the forested mountains, and on the east lie high ridges. Southward, the country opens up revealing Mount Shasta. Once, the air was tainted by the cinnamon bark of Ponderosa pines, but now we are denied its sweetness.

Immediately after the trial, we were advised not to give up hope. A religious group, the Quakers, was trying to help us. People were signing petitions, and it was the Grandfather President Grant who would finally decide our fate.

Yesterday, Colonel Wheaton, the soldier-chief, visited us in our cell and shook our hands. For a moment our hearts sang with hope. But then he frowned and through an interpreter, he told us: 'President Grant has decided that the Modoc renegades must be made an example of, otherwise all Indian tribes will take to the warpath.' He paused, then said: 'You will die tomorrow.'

Wheaton asked Jack if he had any final request. Jack said, 'Yes, I should like to live until I die a natural death.' But we all knew his wish would not be fulfilled.

Presently a chaplain gave us a talk. We listened to him, pretending respect, though I was the only one who understood his words.

Through the iron bars of our window, we

have witnessed the gallows being erected across the square. It has pine poles a foot thick that rise against the sky like a monstrous skeleton. A ladder leads to the platform, and six nooses above the trap await us. Close by are six graves, freshly-heaped earth alongside. 'A new home for you,' one of our guards tells us. But recently we have chosen not to look.

I glance around at my companions. We are dressed in army trousers and striped shirts. We are chained in pairs. Jack has become ghost-thin. The white man dubbed him Captain Jack because he favoured military buttons. He sits with a blanket drawn up, sometimes belching; only his eyes revealed. These no longer show defiance but are dull. The Post Surgeon drugs him with opiates.

The Modocs are not like the plains Indians. We do not wear fancy feathers; in earlier times our clothing consisted of grass, tule fibre, or animal skin. But recently we have worn clothing cast off by whites – levis, store-bought shirts. We care nothing for taking

19

scalps, counting coup or fancy horse-back tricks. Some say we are the poor relations of the Sioux, Comanche, Cheyenne. I don't agree.

Yesterday Jack's wife and daughter visited him in the cell. He clasped the child to his chest while his wife wept. He is not as wicked as the tribunal suggested. Yes, he killed General Canby, but he had no option.

Chained to Jack, is Schonchin John. The terror in his eyes makes him look insane and his head jerks constantly. Perhaps he will be the one who breaks down upon the scaffold. Or will it be me? I have never considered myself brave.

Opposite Schonchin John are the dwarf-like Boston Charley and Black Jim. They are wearing army hats as if intent on dying like bluecoats. Their faces are emotionless. Chained to me is Slolux. He looks uncon-cerned. His brain has gone. Throughout the trial, he showed only boredom, often going to sleep, snoring. Several times the Judge Advocate was obliged to rouse him.

Finally, I consider myself. I believe I am twenty summers old, though I am unsure. A year back, I lost my left eye when a chip of obsidian flew up when I was making an arrow-point. Once I was called Michael. Those who have placed us on trial do not realize that I was born a white man, that I was captured in an Indian raid when I was three and raised as a Modoc. I have not enlightened my captors; I fear that if I reveal the truth, I will be deemed a traitor. By playing an idiot, like Slolux, I hoped to escape the rope, but the officers judging us showed no mercy. I will die as a Modoc.

We stiffen as shouts sound from outside; the guard is being drawn up. I can see that Jack is praying to the spirits but I doubt they will help. We hear keys rattle in locks; the outer doors are being thrown open. Boston Charlie coughs nervously. John Schonchin's head-jerking grows frantic; he fights his chains but they are unrelenting. Our lives are ebbing away. We hear movement in the outer cell, booted footsteps, and then our cell door is opened.

'On your feet!' Sergeant Hardeman shouts. His voice shows a brittle edge not displayed previously. I think he is a merciful man at heart.

We exchange glances. I feel the bitter taste of bile in my throat. We do not move, but a corporal kicks us several times until we climb complainingly to our feet, our legs stiff with cramp, our chains making us clumsy, our hearts as heavy as rock.

We are pushed through the outer room of the guardhouse, and I see the clock on the wall points to nine. It is the appointed time.

The morning is clear. We stand for a moment on the guardhouse stoop, blinking in the sunlight, surprised that so many blue-coats, sweating in their thick uniforms, are formed up in column. All for just six chained prisoners! On the left are musicians, their brass instruments glinting in the sun. They are making a show of our deaths. Before us is a wagon drawn by four horses. It carries pine-wood coffins. Across the square we can see the crowd waiting expectantly, hundreds of people, cordoned back from the gallows by bluecoats. It is a gala day for the white settlers. Many Modoc prisoners are being forced to also watch the executions. We can hear the shocked cries of Modoc women. They are weeping for us. I wonder if my stepmother is there. I look for her, cannot glimpse her.

Beyond the spectators, are the mountains, the pine forests, the blue skies freedom. No different from a million other mornings, apart from the fact that this will be the last we shall see. But what are we? What difference will our deaths make to the passage of this world? I breathe air deep into my lungs. It is hard to believe that I will shortly no longer be breathing.

We are forced up onto the wagon. It is difficult, being chained in pairs. Jack is weak, would fall but for the support of a corporal. Eventually, we sit upon the coffins. They are of finest pine – but they could be of solid gold for all we care. Flies buzz about our heads.

Scarcely are we seated when the officer orders the wagon forward, the wheels creaking. The bluecoats march slowly behind us, their rifles on their shoulders. The band is playing a dirge, the drums muffled. Despite the snail's pace, it seems but seconds before we are across the square and the wagon halts. Excitement is growing in the crowd. Some people are craning their necks to peer at us.

Four dogs, belonging to the garrison, are sprawled beneath the gallows. They are unconcerned by events. How lucky they are!

I believe I am trembling, although I wonder why I do not feel more afraid.

Boston Charley is leaning forward, peering up with morbid interest at the gallows. The bluecoats have formed a three-sided square. On the scaffold platform, bluecoats, holding black hoods in readiness, wait behind chairs upon which the condemned will sit. To one side of the scaffold, is a table. Several men sit at it, scribbling on paper. They are newspaper reporters. Our deaths will make big news.

An officer steps forward, gestures that we

are to dismount from the wagon. As we do so, Jack's blanket slips away. His eyes are sunken deep and he looks more emaciated than ever, but there is no fear in his face, just resignation. Maybe his thoughts are with his wives and little girl. I have no such loved ones, apart from my stepmother and father.

Now two blacksmiths chisel away our chains. It feels strange to be unfettered at last. We stamp our feet, flex our legs. Black Jim is chewing a cud of baccy; he spits contemptuously.

I have heard that in some cases death is immediate at the end of the rope; the neck snaps. In other cases, a man can survive the first drop only to cough and choke slowly to death. I pray that I will be spared that.

A corporal stands with an axe by the rope which holds the trap. It will be he who, with one downward slash, will plunge us into the next world. Slolux looks bewildered. It is too much for his simple brain. John Schonchin shows dizziness, almost falls but is supported by a soldier. He has fouled himself. The smell taints the air. My own bowels are twitching. My trembling is returning – and yet, in my head, I am still not afraid. Perhaps one does not feel fear at the time of danger, only afterwards. If this is so, maybe death will be surprisingly merciful. The chaplain, the sky doctor, stands with a Bible in his hand as he prepares to speak his useless words.

But firstly, the officer called 'adjutant' steps forward, standing stiffly before us. He reads in a pompous voice from a paper, his words being translated into Modoc by a half-breed called Dave Hill – but I understand the English. Its message cuts my breath with shock.

'The executive order dated August 22 1873 approving sentence of death of certain Modoc Indian prisoners is hereby modified in the cases of Slolux and Barncho; and the sentence in said cases is commuted to life imprisonment. Alcatraz Island, Harbor of San Francisco, is designated as the place of confinement.

Signed: U.S. GRANT – President.'

CHAPTER TWO

I cannot recall my white parents; not do I have any resentment against the Indians who perpetrated their deaths. I grew to manhood as a Modoc, respecting my new father and mother. They loved me as their own, never chastising me.

My step-mother was a midwife.

I was always with her, watching with the women who came to see each birth. My mother, forever wearing her basket hat, would instruct the infants' fathers; it was often the practice that they should offer what assistance they could at the time of the delivery.

Sometimes a shaman would also be present, wearing a special bear-claw necklace. He would sing a song and call upon such spirits as Buzzard, Owl and Eagle if the birthing proved difficult. I decided that if I were to be born a woman, I would rather not be born at all.

After a birth, no enquiry was made as to the sex of the child for that was considered impolite.

I do not witness the death of Jack and the others. Slolux and I are returned to the guardhouse. But we hear the thunderous crack when the trap-door collapses beneath the condemned men. The Modocs watching from the stockade unleash an anguished, keening wail – a sound that rises high, probing into the deepest part of my soul. My heart feels like a captive bird, fluttering frantically. Later, a soldier tells me how the corpses of Jack and Black Jim swung easily, while Boston and John Schonchin were gripped by convulsions. Apparently the dogs at the foot of the scaffold remained asleep, undisturbed.

That night my mind is filled with nightmares although my eyes remain open. I am on the scaffold with Jack, a hood over my head, while the noose chokes me.

Next morning Slolux is in bad spirits. He babbles like the idiot he is. He tells me that he expected to die and it is a bad shock to him that he still alive. I do not share his sentiments. He vomits, becomes ill. Shortly, he starts to cough. I am thankful that we are no longer shackled together. Only my wrists remain cuffed.

I feel cowed by what has happened. I experience the fear I should have known yesterday. Sometimes I pinch myself to make certain I am alive. I hear that the bodies of Jack and the others have been decapitated, that their heads will be shipped to Washington and used for what the white man calls 'scientific research'. They seek to discover what makes Indians bad. I wonder what they would have found inside my head. The remains of the corpses are consigned to the graves and the earth is shovelled in. From within our cell, Slolux and I hear the clink of spades on the pebbly earth.

Before Jack died, his hair was shorn so the noose would fit properly. People are paying money for locks of his hair. They will keep them as souvenirs. Perhaps this is no worse than the ghoulishness of the corporal who kept General Canby's false teeth after Jack had killed him.

Slolux becomes more sick. The Post Surgeon says that Slolux must be transferred to the post hospital. A day or so ago they would have choked him to death. Now they are concerned for his health. Even so, I suspect they will chain him to his pallet.

So I am left alone in the cell, for the first time since we were first incarcerated. The sores on my legs throb with pain. But at least the chains have now been removed.

On the fourth day, Sergeant Hardeman visits me. His hair is as white as a winter moon. He limps, still carrying a wound from the great war when the whites fought each other. I do not think he hates me too badly because, after he has blown a great cloud of smoke from his mouth, he allows me to take a draw from his pipe.

'How long before we go to this place Alcatraz?' I ask him.

He looks at me askance. 'You speak American?'

I nod. I think nothing is to be gained by playing the idiot any longer.

'At the agency school,' I say. 'They would not let us speak Modoc – only American.'

I was amongst the first Modoc children to be taught at the Yainax Agency. I recall how they carried out daily roll calls and told us about a holy virgin who had a baby without lying with a man.

After a moment I ask again: 'How long before we go to Alcatraz?'

'Slolux is too ill to travel,' he explains. 'But there is another prisoner coming – a civilian, a bad man. You will travel with him by wagon. You will go tomorrow along the Rancheria Road to Redding and then on to San Francisco. The rest of your tribe are to be moved to a big reservation in the Indian Territories. They will travel on the iron horse. It is a long distance away.'

The iron horse! The thought makes me shudder.

Even so, I say, 'I wish I could go with them.'

Presently my mind swings back to my own future.

'What is Alcatraz like?'

He removes his hat, wipes his brow with the back of his hand. After a moment he says. 'When you see Alcatraz, you will wish you had died with Jack and the others. It is on an island in San Francisco Bay. They say that the waters around it swarm with sharks.'

'Sharks?' I feel alarmed. 'What are sharks?'

'They are big fish. They will eat any man who swims in the water.'

I drop my head, gaze at my feet. Presently my food is brought – meat mixed with sow-belly. I have no hunger. I leave the food upon the floor beside me. Flies buzz about it. When I wave them away, they rise but always return. Eventually, I allow them their fill.

What will this man who is to share my journey to Alcatraz be like? What wicked deeds has he committed? Has he, too, escaped the noose by a hair's breadth?

For the rest of the day I sit, enduring the creep of time. I hide inside my own head. Sometimes my mind goes far back, deep into the darkness of my inner self, leaving my body behind. Much later I emerge from this other world. I hear bluecoats drilling on the parade ground. I peer through my tiny window. They have taken down the gallows. Only the graves remain to mark the spot. Later comes the sound of gunfire. The bluecoats are practising on a rifle range. Maybe soon they will find more Indians to kill.

The man who is to accompany me to Alcatraz arrives late in the evening. I do not see him, his wagon draws up outside the guardhouse. I hear the rattling of his chains. He is placed in the next cell to mine, but a wall separates us. The guards shout orders; he does not answer. Presently, after a bugle sounds 'taps' and the night deepens, I hear this new man coughing and breaking wind. I try to form an image of him in my mind, but I cannot – apart from the belief that he is a giant. In contrast, I myself have somehow inherited the trait of most Modocs. I am short, slightly bandy. I guess I will be chained to this new man tomorrow when we start our journey. He will overshadow me.

Next morning I feed early. Fried salt pork, chewy as leather, beans, corn bread, sorghum. I wolf it down, using my fingers. I scald my mouth with coffee. My appetite has returned. I can feel the air coming through the bars of my window, keen as a blade. There is heavy frost, but I know heat will come later. It is October with its frosty mornings, gradually changing to the shimmering heat of mid-morning. It is still dark when two bluecoats unlock my cell. I am forced to relieve myself, then they fix handcuffs around my wrists, their hands impatient.

I am pushed into the corridor and for the first time I see my fellow prisoner. He

34

reminds me of a bear. His face has a steel-trap look about it, with low, deep-lined forehead and eyes that seem too small for his skull. His hair hangs down only to his shoulders; it has been hacked off, probably by a prison barber. I guess he is maybe fifty. I believe that if he attempts to escape from Alcatraz, these sharks better watch out, for it will be he who does the eating, not them. In the dim light I feel his eyes touch me contemptuously. We do not talk. As we are shackled together, I can feel the muscle in his leg. I can also feel hatred radiating from him. He clearly resents being chained to an Indian. I do not enlighten him in any way. Legs locked together with the connecting chain, one of us has to step forward with his right leg, while the other advances with his left and so on, otherwise we would trip and fall, and I do not fancy his weight on top of me. I hear one of the guards curse him and call him. 'Angry Zeb Buller.'

Another man says, 'Bet he's angry now all right!' and there is an explosion of laughter amongst the guards which is cut off by an impatient grunt from Sergeant Havers. They would not laugh if Buller were free. The bluecoats have bandoleers of shells strapped around them and they are all carrying Spencer carbines.

As we wait, a bugle heralds reveille, rousing those members of the garrison who still slumber. Soon will come the usual routine of roll call, breakfast, sick call, guard mount and the adjutant's call. Hopefully I will never again see these buildings of Fort Klamath – the commissary storehouse, guardhouse, stables, barrack rooms. The thought causes me no grief.

Lanterns glow in front of the Commander's Headquarters and, through the mistiness, I see a wagon awaiting, the driver on the seat looking like a gnome. Four mules stand patiently in their shaft-harness. The wagon resembles a big box, some twelve feet long, fashioned from hardwood plank. At the rear are double doors with slidebolts and a step, and on its sides are lashed water kegs. It has iron-tired wheels. It reminds me of a white man's hearse.

Bluecoats are rushing about in the morning gloom, orders being shouted. Some are mounted on horses; the breath of men and animals comes in freezing white plumes. I am thankful that I have a blanket around my shoulders.

Zeb Buller and I are pushed forward. Hampered by our chains, we stumble, almost fall. The rawness of my legs makes me clench my teeth to prevent from crying out. Bluecoats swear at us, hovering around like flies. My companion remains silent and I struggle to match his stride. He does not care about me. He will drag me along the ground if I go down, but I stay on my feet and shortly we reach the wagon and the door at its rear is opened.

We are bundled up the step, pushed inside. Behind us the door is slammed shut; the bolts are slid across. Zeb Buller lowers his hulk to the floor and I drop down beside him. Then we wait for a long time before orders are shouted from outside, a whip cracks, and the wagon lurches forward, its iron-tired wheels biting jarringly into ground. I know we have a strong escort – six bluecoats, under the command of a Sergeant Havers.

There is a small vent in the roof of our vehicle. Through this I can see the sky. The lightness of the new day strengthens. As the sun radiates, early warmth drives away the frigidity of dawn. The vent appears to provide our only air. I wonder if we will suffocate. Within an hour, all frost and fog will have vanished. Our prison will become like a sweat box.

I have heard that our journey will take a week.

CHAPTER THREE

I recall when the Rancheria Road was built. Many summers back, I watched as the ring of axes sounded. Bluecoats and civilians felled the giant redwood trees and pushed boulders aside to cleave a passage south towards a town called Redding with its log houses, saloons and gambling houses and then westward to another town – Shasta. It was near here that the white men, hair-faces, first discovered yellow iron. Hordes invaded Mawatoc in their canvas-covered bone-shakers. They searched everywhere for gold, working with shovels, pans and rockers, scaring away the game. Soon settlers began building cabins. Resentment flared and thus began the confrontation between hair-faces and Indians. The whites spread sickness and left poisoned food for the Indians to find.

Eventually hatred led to the murder of General Canby, Captain Jack's execution and my own imprisonment.

But today I have no sight of the surrounding country, for I sit sweating within the gloomy wagon as it jolts over potholes. Presently I lapse into torpor, allow the hours to flow past. Much later, I glance at Zeb Buller's steel-trap face and I am shocked. I see the glint of his teeth. He is grinning – almost, it seems, with satisfaction. Why? And there is something else – the smell of his sweating body has gone up a notch. Afterwards I will swear, that he knew the exact point of the trail we had reached and foresaw the deadly sequence of events which was to unfold.

A thunderous fusillade of gunfire bludgeons our ears, and with it, from outside, the panicking shouts of men and the screaming of animals. The wagon shudders, skews sideways, almost topples over. Zeb Buller and I are hurled across its floor like flotsam, his weight crunching the wind from me as we are slammed against the side. The shots continue – rapid rifle fire from all around. Bullets are striking the exterior of the wagon. It seems all hell has descended on us. At last the gunfire trails off to be replaced by the groaning of men and animals.

Into the singing echo of it all, I hear voices that I have not heard before, and other voices are crying out for mercy. With them comes the erratic snap of hand-guns. Clearly wounded men are being despatched. I clamp my own mouth shut, wish I could vanish into nowhereness.

Zeb Buller does not stir. I am pinned beneath him, soaked in both his sweat and my own. His breathing is ragged. There is something of expectation about him as if he knows what will happen next.

A minute passes, or is it an hour? My awareness is muddled. Then the bolts on the wagon door are drawn back, the door swings open and sunlight lances around us. We are no longer alone. Boots thud on the wagon's floor. I keep my face down. The air is tainted by the smell of those who are climbing in. Gradually I allow myself to glance up. There are several men, hair-faces, thick-shoul-dered, swarthy. Maybe Mexicans.

Zeb Buller struggles impatiently. 'Get me free!' he shouts and he jerks savagely against the chain that links our legs, causing me pain but I remain silent.

One of the newcomers says: 'Where's the key!'

'Damn the key,' Zeb Buller growls. 'Kill him, then cut his leg off!'

Am I about to enter the black-velvet night of the spirit-land? I am aware that a man is standing over me, a pistol in his hand. I try to twist away, but the chain about my ankle, anchored by Zeb Buller's weight, restricts me. I gaze up into the black eye of the gun, as helpless as a beast awaiting slaughter.

But all at once a voice sounds from out-side the wagon, slicing through the pant of men's breathing.

'I 'ave the keys!' and I hear the rattling of the bunch, and I realize that they must have been snatched from the belt of the sergeant.

Of the three hair-faces who crowded into the wagon, two clamber out to make space, and a further man, a tangled beard to his waist, scrambles in brandishing the keys. The gun pointed at my head wavers and then is withdrawn as rough hands grapple with our ankle chain.

'Hurry!' Zeb Buller cries.

It seems to take an age. The hands of the man with the keys are clumsy. I fear that he will lose his patience and cut my leg off after all. He tries three keys before he finds the right one. He turns it and the pressure of the chain slackens. Zeb Buller is on his feet in an instant, seeming not caring that his head bangs against the wagon's roof.

'And my hands,' he demands, holding up his linked wrists. A further turn of a key has him completely free. His scornful eyes touch me. 'Kill the Indian!' he shouts as he leaps through the doorway of the wagon, followed by the long-bearded one. I am left with the man who was about to blow my brains out a minute earlier. I notice he has a snake band about his hat. Now he raises his pistol again, steadies it on his forearm, grinning fiendishly.

I am flushed with urgent strength. I brace my shoulders against the wooden planking and kick my leg in a scything arc, the chain slamming my would-be killer across the face. He is thrown back, showering me with his blood. I scramble across the floor like a frantic crab, my senses finding new sharpness. I grab the fallen pistol – a big Navy colt. My hands, still linked by chain, are slippery with sweat – but somehow I aim the weapon, my finger curled inside the triggerguard. His grimacing face is streaming with blood. As I fire the pistol leaps within my fist and fills the wagon with ear-singing blast.

I fall back knowing that I have killed him. He is sprawled across my legs, a bloody soup of brain matter seeping from the bullet hole in his forehead. I crouch, shudders flowing through my body, the smoking gun still in my manacled hands. I spin its chamber, thumb back the hammer, expecting the return of Zeb Buller and his rescuers. I steady my breath, try to listen, but the blast from the shot I fired still deafens me to other sound.

Maybe they have gone away. Maybe they think the shot that sounded killed me, not their man, and are departing. But surely at any moment my enemies will miss their companion and come back to seek him. My wrists are still linked and one end of the chain remains attached to my ankle. Chain has saved my life, but now I wish I could be rid of it. I extract my legs from beneath the dead man. His face no longer exists. With the gun ready in my hands, I steady myself in the doorway, then cautiously glance out. The noon sun is scorching, flaring in the sky like a white scream. My one-eyed vision is blurred with sweat. Everything before me shimmers as if in a giddy film of water. My ears still ring with the blast of gunfire, but gradually this is replaced by what at first I think is silence. Then I realize that it is not silence. It is a steady roar made by the wing-beats of myriads of feasting flies. As I crouch, poised in the wagon's doorway, they swirl about me. I raise my cuffed hands, wave them away. I wipe my eye with my sleeve. My mind takes in the scene. Crumpled bodies; bloody, bullet-torn uniforms and faces still reflecting agony. Horses and mules are sprawled lifeless. Fly-encrusted blood forms dark pools upon the trail.

Even during the Modocs battle against the bluecoats in the Lava Beds I never saw such carnage and this knowledge has me stumbling back into the wagon and slumping beside the man I have killed. I feel no pity for the bluecoats. A few suns ago they would have hanged me.

Zeb Buller's gang must have been waiting. They caught the wagon in ambush, shooting down its six-man escort. Those men who did not die immediately were killed with a bullet to the head, their pleading eyes drawing no mercy.

I sit in stunned inactivity, the unmistakable smell of gore, of death, thickening the air.

Why have I survived? Firstly I escaped the hang-rope, now I have survived this on-slaught. Do the spirit-gods grant me special favours after all?

Gradually my senses steady, then my gaze pauses on the bunch of keys close to my feet. I place the pistol down and grasp them. My hands shake, but at the third attempt I find the key that fits the lock of the chain still attached to my ankle. The key is rusty, but at last it twists and I shake the chain clear. The next task is even more difficult. I try four keys from the bunch before I find one that fits my handcuffs. I work frantic-ally, inserting it, attempting to twist it. It is tricky because my wrists are still linked and all the time I have the feeling that Zeb Buller and his killers will return and exact vengeance.

At last the cuff slips away from my wrists, drops to the floor. I must get away from here. Life is still precious to me, no matter what torment it offers. Now, at least, I am free of the chains.

I retrieve the gun. My body feels immensely heavy as I clamber onto my feet. I drop from the wagon, landing on all fours. I see how the mules are lying dead in the harness. Everywhere the flies swarm thickly.

I straighten up, stumble forward, half falling over the corpse of a soldier, I sense a shadow passing over me and hear the flapping of wings. Greedy turkey-vultures, four of them, descend from the sky – are landing and tucking in their scrawny, white-trimmed wings as they strut towards the bodies.

I must get away. If Zeb Buller and his murderers do not return, then other white men will come, maybe bluecoats, and they will offer no mercy. They will be convinced that I have taken part in the killings. I must escape into the obscurity of the trail-side trees.

It is now the voice comes.

I spin round, gun raised. Sprawled on his side against the front wagon wheel is

Sergeant Havers, the chief of the escort party. He is a grey-haired veteran with what was once a fine handlebar moustache, but now he is scarcely recognizable. His cheek is smashed like an eggshell. He raises his hand, displaying bloody stumps. Two of his fingers have been hacked off, taken, I am certain, for the rings they bore. A sudden bout of coughing rakes him. His eyes are pleading with me.

I glance about, still fearful that my enemies will return, but nothing has changed in the surrounding trees. I go to the wounded man. He tries to speak. I kneel down, place my ear close to his lips and hear the word ... *water!*

I am sure he is the only survivor.

Why should I care about this man? He has done little for me. Even so I look around, see a canteen on the ground. I scrabble across to it and curse. It has been pierced by a bullet, its content drained out. I recall that there are barrels of water attached to the wagon's sides. Have they been punctured by bullets? Carrying the canteen I check the barrels. One is perforated, but the other is unscathed. I twist its faucet, rip the cork from the canteen and fill it up to the level of the bullet hole. I return to the sergeant. He is still conscious, though only just. I fan the flies away, press the canteen to his lips and allow a slow trickle to enter his mouth, then I withdraw it as coughing rakes his body. When he recovers I allow him some more water. His eyes centre on my face.

'Why...?' he whispers. 'Why do you help m-me?'

I do not answer. I shake my head and wonder what I should do with him. I feel a desperate desire that he should not die. I cannot explain why. But there is no way that I can convey him back to the fort – and if I wait here until others come, I will be blamed, strung up to the nearest tree or maybe shot. But I put such thoughts from my head, and crouch beside this man, allowing him sips of water when he can take it. At last he rests back.

I gaze up at the towering redwoods alongside the trail. Zeb Buller and his gang seem long gone. Perhaps they have not missed the man I killed. Not far away, the vultures are squabbling over the corpses, their thrusting beaks seeking the entrails. Of course, sooner or later, somebody will appear and discover what has happened. Then the army will be informed and they will go crazy, just as they did after Canby was killed.

My gaze moves over the fly-encrusted bodies. My Indian friends would have been proud of this ambush, bluecoats and animals must have been killed simultaneously. Why Sergeant Havers lives is a mystery.

I could lift him onto my back, maybe carry him to the nearest settlement, leave him where others can find him. But I doubt he would survive a journey. Alternatively, I could wait with him until somebody comes along the trail. Perhaps Sergeant Havers would have a good word for me, but I know I will be sent to Alcatraz anyway and that thought fills me with dread.

Then I notice something.

CHAPTER FOUR

Havers's breathing is growing weaker. I see how his fingernails have become embedded in his palms in his struggle for life. It seems that he like the others is passing into the spirit land. He is doing me a good turn.

I stand up and from the body of a soldier I remove a bandoleer of bullets and slip it around my shoulders. I also take his knife. I cannot find bullets for the revolver, so I throw it aside and gather up a fallen carbine. I work its mechanism, find it undamaged.

Suddenly alarm cuts through me.

I hear an approaching roar … wagons coming along the trail! For the moment they are hidden by the trail's curve. I must run.

Even as I start for the trees, I hear somebody shout, 'My God!' And other shocked voices are raised. I realize I have been spotted and a gun blasts off.

The sight of a man fleeing from the scene of such carnage can do little else but draw a bullet. Lead splinters the bark of a tree to my side and I plunge immediately into the shadowy pines, kicking my way through thorny berry bushes. I run, aware of the sharp pine needles beneath my soles. I run until my lungs are bursting. Finally I collapse to my hands and knees, panting like a dog and listen. Men are shouting and scrambling after me. They sound close. I must force my way on. Doubled over, stumbling, I stagger beneath the canopy of redwoods.

Should they catch me, my guilt will seem confirmed by the desperation of my flight and I will be despatched quicker than a bull at slaughter. Above my head ravens are squawking as if they wish to carry word of my progress.

At least in the trees, nobody will get a clear shot at me, but my weeks of imprisonment have left me weak and I hope that whoever is behind me will turn back before long. My pace grows slower, weariness stiffening my muscles. I spot a big hollow tree, drag myself into its interior and tumble down. Red-devil ants are indignant at my intrusion. The forest is vibrant with the chatter of chipmunks, the chirping of birds. I listen for sound of pursuit, but hear nothing untoward.

When my breathing steadies, I quit my concealment and move on, pausing frequently, straining my ears. Eventually I feel sure that my pursuers have turned back and are busy coming to terms with the remains of the ambush. Retribution will come later.

Much later I find an animal-wallow in the forest floor. It smells of wild hog. I drop into it. Above the high fronds, the sun has lost its fierceness. It must be evening. I rest for an hour or more, feeling the heat leave the day. My strength is returning and still there is no sound of pursuit. What am I going to do? It will be foolish to venture near any settlements for I will be a wanted man, and a quick bullet will leave no reproach; good riddance to an Indian killer who should have gone to the rope anyway. I guess playing the fool stood me in good stead. The grandfather, President Grant, must have considered that nobody without a brain could be guilty of crimes that warranted a hanging, so at the flick of his pen, he'd signed the declaration that had spared my life. But now my acting must be left behind. I must become as crafty as a coyote.

My future seems grim. For well nigh all my conscious life I have lived as an Indian, my white ancestry forgotten. I was treated with all the kindness that the Modocs afforded their own children, and I loved my foster parents far more than I ever loved my unrecalled true parents.

The Modoc tribe was split into several branches. It was with Captain Jack's Lost River Band that I grew up. But now Jack and other leaders are dead, and the remaining people have been moved to the distant land called Oklahoma. My foster parents are now infirm, my father is blind and my mother crippled with rheumatism. Will I ever see them again?

My chances of crossing hundreds of miles to find them is nigh impossible and without doubt somebody would realize that I'm an escaped prisoner and hand me over to the authorities.

So what will I do?

I ponder as the night darkens. I feel the harsh bite of the cold and wish I still had my blanket. Eventually, I decide that I must seek out the white friends whom I can trust – the Emerson family: Bob and Lilly, their daughter Caroline and their son Billy. During the recent summers I worked at their homestead on the north side of Tule Lake, building fences, tilling the soil. They will not betray me. Mrs Emerson once told me that they loved me like a son.

With the butt of the carbine I scrape deeper into my wallow. I curl into it, trying to find warmth from within myself. I hear the hoot of an owl and bats whirr close overhead. Through the branches, I can see the moon, bright as a polished medal. There is a biting sting in the air, the fore runner of the big white face, the winter. My teeth click with the cold, but presently I sleep, and entwined with that slumber comes a dream of years past, of the time we lived on the Klamath reservation.

Old Man Schonchin was chief of the Modocs then, but he lost the respect of Captain Jack and other sub-chiefs like Hooker Jim. Also, there was much resentment against the reservation authorities. Old Man Schonchin did not look after his people. He preferred to turn the other cheek. I recall how Jack's face burned with fury, how in exasperation he and Hooker Jim finally broke away, led our band off the reservation and we walked until we came to the banks of Lost River. As I grew to manhood we hunted freely across the land. But things changed when the bluecoats came, ordering us back to the agency.

I am awake long before dawn, casting my dreams aside, rising, working my stiff limbs. There is frost in the air. Dawn is a shell-pink lever placed between night and the horizon. Soon I am trudging onward through the forest. I am weak with hunger. I am reminded of the time when, as a youth, I went on a quest. I entered a half-dream land where explosive gases and molten, rust-coloured cinders rose from the earth. It was inhabited by spirits and I had been warned not to go there. But teetering on starvation, wisdom had deserted me. I was lucky to escape alive.

Now, I fear my weakened state may carry me there again.

So food is a priority, but I am reluctant to risk a shot in case somebody is stalking me. I reach a stream. I scoop water up in my hands. It is Modoc belief that if your lips drink direct from the stream, you will be inviting illness from the frog-spirit.

I try to think clearly. I know the Emersons will offer me temporary safety. They are good people. I have seen them kneeling together, praying to their god. All my immediate hopes rest with them.

I move cautiously, leave the forest behind

and reach low hills. I am about to cross a small valley when I hear the blowing of horses, the jingle of harness, and my heart misses a beat. I glance around for cover, spot some low rocks, rush to them and drop down. I hug the ground as a column of bluecoats appears, riding in twos. They are weary and dusty, their uniforms stained with sweat. They are coming directly towards me. I decide I will have to make a run for it; they will be sure to find me. They come so close, I can see the angry expressions on their faces, the way their eyes dart all around. They are sure to be furious at the fate of the escort party. They will show no mercy to those they consider guilty. At the last moment, their officer waves them onward down the valley. Only when they have disappeared do I resume steady breathing. I could so easily have been caught in the open.

In the afternoon, I reach Tule Lake and at last risk a shot, bringing down a mule deer that was at the water's edge. Using sticks and twigs, I create a fire, skin and cook the beast and appease my hunger.

It is as I move on that I discover tracks. Six, hard-ridden unshod horses. The tracks have not been left by bluecoats. They are heading around the north side of the lake. My heart sinks; instinct tells me that these tracks have been left by Buller and his men. I must warn the Emersons that dangerous outlaws are roaming close.

It seems I travel forever, forcing my way through the heavy sagebrush which sometimes rises above the shoulders. The sky is grey, the weather forlorn and cold, matching my spirits. A wind is getting up. I do not follow the tracks, but I have seen enough of them to realize that hours ago these men rode eastward along the north side of the lake. My fear deepens. The terrain is familiar; I have traversed it many times before. At last I come clear of the sagebrush and in front of me the ground is open and flat. Some sheep are grazing the grass – the Emersons' flock – and two horses. I notice there are a number of dead animals, lying like grey stones. I guess in a burst of deviltry somebody has shot them. In the centre of the meadow is the Emersons' box-like house and the adjacent small barn. The cabin is made of logs, has a board-roof covered with sod, and a barn for storage.

The ground on the left side has been used for cultivation. In the past I've worked on it for many hours with Mr Emerson. But today there is something strangely different about the place. It brings a chill to my guts.

I hold the carbine ready and step forward. There is no movement anywhere, apart from the two horses within the corral. My fear increases. Twenty yards clear of the small-holding, I call out: 'Mr and Mrs Emerson, it's Barncho!'

I restrain my breathing, listen. Nothing. I cross the intervening space, move around the side of the barn to its opening. And then the familiar smell touches my nostrils. Death! My eye adjusts to the shadowed interior and suddenly I see him. Mr Emerson has been lynched. His body is two feet off the ground, dangling at the end of a rope thrown over a crossbeam. Already flies are buzzing about the corpse. I feel sickened. Mr Emerson has been a good friend to me. I tremble with anger. Why couldn't I have got here before Buller spread his murder?

I find a milking stool. I climb upon it, cut Mr Emerson down, catching his dead weight as it falls. Gently I rest him in the straw. I see how his scalp has been sliced off, but I am sure it has not been done by an Indian for it is a deed of crude butchery. I wonder if it was done while he still lived. I pray to Kumookumts for his soul. I am filled with fury and black hatred.

I cross to the cabin, grimly sensing what I will find. I try the door; it is unlocked. Stepping inside, I see that the place has been ransacked, furniture, clothing and belongings strewn about haphazardly. But it is the sight of Mrs Emerson that draws my eyes. She is lying across the table upon which I enjoyed so many suppers. She is spread-eagled, hands strapped to the table legs, her dress lifted up about her head. Her lips are drawn back in terrible grimace; her once pretty face is twisted with the panic of her final moments. Her body is exposed, bruised, bloody. *You are like a son to us, Barncho,* she once said to me. Grinding my teeth with anguish, I cut the ropes that bind her. I pull her dress over her body, fan away the flies. Even Hooker Jim and his Modoc raiders never harmed women and children when they had attacked the cabins of settlers.

In the second room, I find the bodies of the children sprawled across the beds. Both are dead. The girl, eleven years old, has been mutilated. The younger boy has had his throat cut, his head nigh severed. The last time I saw them, they were smiling and calling farewell to me as I headed back for the camp on Lost River, turning, waving, not dreaming that I would never see them alive again. What tragedy has occurred since that time! Now, the smell is thickening the air.

I stand, choked by grief, my breathing shallow, the only sounds the buzz of flies and the solid tick-tock of the grandfather clock that had been a prized possession. If only I could have got here sooner. We could have barricaded ourselves in, fought the intruders off. There is no doubt in my mind: Buller and his gang have done this. Hatred for them pulses through every part of my body.

I should bury these good folk, but I know I have no time. Sooner or later others will come here and I dare not be discovered. Instead, I must find Buller and his gang, make them pay for what has happened. That is the most important task left to me.

CHAPTER FIVE

Everything of value has been taken from the cabin, apart from one loaf of bread which I eat. I also discover an old coat of Mr Emerson's, considered worthless by the murderers. I put it on, glad of the extra warmth. I glance around the cabin for the final time, say a prayer to Kumookumts for the souls of this family. Others must do the burying of these good folk. Others who are not hounded by the threat of death. I guess Buller has murdered the Emersons as retaliation against the whites for his capture. He must pay the penalty. He may be able to elude the army and civil law, but I will do my utmost to ensure he will not escape me.

In the corner of the barn I find a saddle and bridle; then I go down to the corral and catch the stronger of the two horses, a stockingfoot sorrel, and throw the saddle over his back, slip the bit into his mouth and fix the harness. I think these horses must have belonged to Buller and his gang, but they have swapped them for horses owned by the Emersons, which will have been fresher. However, this sorrel will provide my legs with much-needed respite.

It is growing darker. The low clouds have grown as sullen as my mood. Rain is spitting down like ice-cold tears. I curse it because it will wash out the tracks left by Buller. But at least record of the gang's departure, as they strike eastward, is still easy enough to find. Astride the sorrel I follow tracks along the north side of Tule Lake. The ducks are settling upon the water, preparing themselves for the storm. For what remains of that wet day I follow the dwindling trail. But by the time dusk is closing in I can no longer see any sign. I dismount and find a spot near the lake where the cottonwoods cluster. I unsaddle and hobble the stockingfoot and seek shelter for myself.

During the night I am aware that the storm worsens, but my entire being is far too restless with hatred for Buller for it to worry me. I only hope that come daylight I will find some indication of the direction they have taken. As early light streaks the eastern sky I am on my way. I spot broken grass stems, horse droppings; and mid-morning I discover where they made camp for the night. I am sure that there are six of them, but I am dismayed to see that they have split up, three heading westward, while the remainder continued southward around the lake. More than ever my hatred rests on Buller himself. However evil his companions are, I am certain that he is guilty of the worst depravity. I suspect that today some passserby or even an army patrol will discover the Emerson bodies. The hunt for Buller will grow even more determined, and for me too. I will be judged as they are judged. My own eventual fate seems almost no longer important. But I am determined not to be caught before I have avenged the murders of my friends.

Despite searching for sign of Buller himself, I am unable to find indication as to which group he has accompanied. I have to take a chance. I decide to follow the tracks going around the lake, heading towards the area that the Modocs call the Land of the Burned Out Fires. This is the terrain that was our sacred land, a vast area of extinct volcanoes and lava flows, where the rocks are as sharp as razors and honeycombed with caves and crevices.

To the white man, it is a waterless, treeless, volcanic hell. This was the area into which Jack led us after the bluecoats attacked us at Lost River. We had crossed the stormy Tule Lake and found refuge in the great crescent of rocks that lies in the heart of this malpais. It is a natural defensive postion. It was from here that for six months our people withstood the might of the United States Army, sheltering in the caves from a bombardment of cannon fire, repelling the attacks of the bluecoats. As long as our ammunition and food supplies held up, which we obtained by nightly raids onto neighbouring ranch land, there is little doubt that we could have remained there for much longer. But Jack and Hooker Jim fell out after the killing of the general.

Jack knew of a secluded cleft that would take us through the army lines, and it was in the dead of night our exodus was made. Once free, Jack and Hooker Jim led their respective supporters in different directions. I, together with my Modoc parents, went with Jack and we were many miles eastwards before the bluecoats discovered our departure.

Now the thought is growing in me that the three men I am following who hopefully include Buller himself, are striking out for the now deserted Stronghold hoping that they will find refuge there. I convince myself of this prospect, but I have nothing to support it, for as I travel all evidence of their progress has been washed out by the rain. I pray to Kumookumts that he will guide me, but Buller and his companions could have disappeared anywhere into this country.

By the following morning I have reached the land of the Lava Beds and I know I will have to discard the sorrel. His hoofs would soon be cut to shreds on the sharp rocks. I will once again have to rely on my own feet. I unsaddle him, slap his rump and give him his freedom. I know that if my guesswork is wrong, I will regret this action, but if my enemies are at hand the presence of a horse will give me away. It is a chance I have to take.

When it is dark again, I make my precarious way across the three miles of rocks towards the Stronghold. My hands and feet suffer many cuts, but my main concern is to quell all sound of my progress and to ensure that the carbine does not rattle against the rocks. I am thankful that the night sky is low and shrouded by cloud. The rain has relented to a steady drizzle.

I clamber onward and the ground dips down and ahead the rocky ramparts of the

Stronghold show. I move with the confidence of memory and enter the Stronghold near the old juniper tree that has always served as a landmark. The only other vegetation here, in these barren rocks, consists of clumps of sagebrush and bunch grass. In the centre of the Stronghold is a great crater-like pit, big enough for a large wickiup; it is surrounded by fissures and caverns, which form a network of natural trenches and dugouts. The rocks are piled up in semi circular fashion with view holes through which we fired our guns. We built breastworks to fill in the few gaps left by nature in these fortifications. The place has dozens of connecting caves, pot holes formed when the lava boiled, and many dangerous pitfalls. But I believe I have one great advantage over my quarry, if they have sought shelter here. I lived here for six months, and am acquainted, even if blindfolded, with every rocky pathway and cave. If they are present, I convince myself I will find them.

But now dank darkness is deepening. I

strain my senses for anything that will reveal the presence of my quarry. All I hear is the hooting of an owl and in the far distance the bark of a coyote. I hope the coyote will not follow me, for in Modoc eyes that would be a sign of my impending doom.

Maybe I am completely wrong. Buller and his gang, perhaps split, could be a hundred miles away by now. Alternatively, maybe the bluecoats have caught them, and subjected them to the punishment they deserve. But I think it is doubtful.

For an hour, maybe two, I prowl Nature's dark alleyways, hoping for some sign. The rocks, unyielding and sharp, seem like old friends. I slip along the paths, through the crevices, like a ghost. But I am over-confident, because carelessly I reach into a crevice and my fingers touch dry scales. Instinctively I know this is a rattlesnake, thick in the middle, coiled in its hibernation. I snatch my hand back. Another second and its muscles might have contracted to send deadly spit into my bloodstream.

I pass the dark shadow of the cave where my family sheltered from the bombardment of the army. Two teenaged Modoc boys were blasted to bits by cannon balls. They were our sole casualties during the entire campaign. But now there only remain scars in the rock to indicate the bombardment. And there is nothing in the darkness to imply other than that I am the only human-being present in the Stronghold. I am weary; I have had a long day of travel and need to sleep. I decide to conserve my energy until daylight and rest down in a rocky crevice. I am close to the entrance of the cave that Jack used. In front of it is a slab of rock which he stood upon when he spoke to the people.

I ensure my carbine is charged. I am cold and wet, but hunched in my coat, it is not long before I lapse into sleep.

I dream of the old days, when we kept watch for the bluecoats from Nature's ramparts, and of the day when the great attack came, the blue coats swarming across the rocks towards us. Crouched down behind our fortifications we waited until they were close, then we opened fire. They were without cover, helpless to shield themselves from our bullets, while their fire did nothing but chip the rock surroundings. The fight did not last long, soon they were scrambling back towards their camp at the base of the far ridge. When they had gone, our women went out and took the guns, ammunition and clothing from the dead bluecoats. It was a day of triumph for the Modocs.

Any satisfaction that my dream gives me is suddenly shattered. I come awake, sensing menace. For a second I lay aware only of the beat of my heart. And then the voice comes.

'Don't move or I kill you!'

I smell gun oil in the cold, dank air.

For the time of five heart-beats I remain perfectly still. I can hear the ragged breathing of this man who has come upon me and curse myself for allowing myself to be surprised. Then I realize that my hand is upon the carbine, my finger curled inside

74

the trigger guard.

In one frenzied motion, I throw myself over and fire into the shadow looming above me. For an instant I see his face illuminated in orange glow, then it is gone. My assailant makes no sound; his presence has been blasted away. I scramble up, see him in the dim light sprawled motionless a few yards away. I can smell his blood. I know he will not trouble me further. Once again I have achieved a narrow escape. My reasoning was correct. My quarry, at least some of them, has sought refuge here in the Stronghold. But where are the others?

I have to shift my position. If they are close the shot will have alerted them. I move silently along the dark gallyway. After several minutes, I pause, crouch down, listen. I can no longer smell the acrid taint of gunfire or blood but gradually another smell enters my nostrils. Woodsmoke! There are a number of caves surrounding me. I feel sure that somebody is burning a campfire in one of them. Whoever it is will have heard the gunshot.

To my right is the cave that was once occupied by Hooker Jim, and I gaze towards it and catch the faintest glimmer of flame from within. My veins are tingling. I wish there was more light, but even so I can make out the black opening of the cave and I'm sure that I will be able to see any movement that occurs. I know that there is no way out at the back of the cave. If curiosity draws anybody to investigate, they will prove an easy target for me. I notice that the faint glow of the fire has been snubbed out.

To my reckoning, there should be two men inside. I pray that one of them is Buller. Thought of him brings images into my mind, images of Mr Emerson and his family brutally killed, and angry bile rises into my throat.

But I wait and time slips away with no person emerging from the cave. My enemies are crafty. I must remain alert, prevent them escaping from the cave. My patience must be greater than theirs. Sooner or later one of us will make the mistake of moving and in so doing be at the mercy of the other. My head still aches with weariness. I know that if I close my eyes I may lapse into slumber and then anything can happen. If I had salt I would rub it into my eye to keep it open, but I have no salt.

I crouch down with my carbine aimed at the cave opening. I wish I could see into the gloomy depths and discover if my enemies are hiding there. The coyote has grown silent at last and the owl is finished with its night's hunt. I notice the glimmer of light in the eastern sky and know that another dawn will soon emerge.

And then suddenly my enemy shows himself.

CHAPTER SIX

He appears like a snail slithering from his hole. All I see in the gloom are his head and shoulders, but it provides the target I seek. Aiming carefully, I fire the carbine. My enemy is thrown back, disappears into the shadows. Like his earlier compatriot I know that he is done for. I feel elated. For a brief moment my heart sings, but then I realize that my work is not finished. Neither of the men I have killed is Buller. I reason that there is one of my enemies left inside the cave, but it may not be Buller. I curse. I have been incredibly lucky so far. Maybe now my luck has run out. And then another doubt plagues me. Perhaps the cave is now empty apart from the body of the dead man. Maybe the third man, whether he is Buller or not, is elsewhere in the Stronghold. If so, he will have heard the gunshots and may be, even at this moment, stalking me!

I glance around uneasily. The light is growing stronger, but my view is restricted by the rock walls. I make a decision: I will have to go into the cave, face my remaining enemy if he is there.

I straighten up. I have slipped another bullet into the breach of the carbine, silently pulled back the bolt. With the weapon ready, I start to advance, gingerly stepping forward over the rocks, not knowing whether I am observed, not knowing whether I will be dead within seconds. The dark entrance of the cave looms in front of me and soon I am stepping over the body of the man I have killed. His blood is splattered across the rock floor. I pause, again seeking sign that I am not alone.

Bent low, I creep forward. I feel the warmth of the ashes that so recently were a campfire. Its remains are surrounded by a few blankets, discarded food cans and some empty bottles. It dawns on me. I am alone in this cave. The very emptiness sends a chill deep through me. If my third enemy is around, he is roving elsewhere in the Stronghold. The thought is chilling. He, like I was so recently, may well have his gun aimed at the entrance of the cave. Our positions have been reversed. Have I made a terrible mistake?

I examine the body of the man I have killed. He is unmistakably a Mexican and I am sure he was one of those who attacked the escort party. My bullet took him clean between the eyes, blowing a hole in the back of his skull, ejecting his brain.

Now, the longer I remain in this cave, the greater the danger. The body I have left lying in the mouth of the cave will be visible from outside. I must drag it back into the shadowy interior; in so doing I may present myself as a target. I wonder if this was the man who tortured my good friends. I do not regret killing him. Or the other man. They deserve their fate. I pray that Buller will also suffer.

I rapidly drag the dead man back into the shadows. I check through his pockets. All I find is a small necklace. It was one of the few treasures that Mrs Emerson possessed, bearing a picture of a beautiful goddess. This man must have torn it from her as he subjected her to his brutality. I slip the necklace into my pocket. I will keep it as a reminder of this woman who was so kind to me. Had she not been the wife of another man, I would gladly have given her my love, although I am sure she looked upon me as a youngster who had not yet reached maturity.

Now once again I carefully study the rocks outside the cave. The rain has stopped but the day is still gloomy. Nothing moves within my vision. Where is Buller? Is he somewhere out there, watching the cave entrance, waiting for a chance to shoot me? My doubts return. Perhaps Buller is a hundred miles away; perhaps I am skulking here in vain, frightened by my own shadow. Whatever the situation, I determine to bring matters to a head. I take a deep breath, then make my way swiftly out of the cave entrance, trigger finger poised.

But there is no blast of gunfire, no sudden

slam of lead into my guts. I move away from the cave, using rocks as cover. I gaze around at the higher pinnacles. I tense as a bird flaps skywards, but apart from that … nothing.

I curse Buller. Where on God's earth is he? Is he somewhere within the Stronghold, hiding, waiting?

And then the shot comes.

I feel the impact against my upper chest, am slammed back into a deep fissure at the side. My head cracks against rock; I am stunned and dizzy, yet grimly aware that I've been hit and outwitted.

As my head clears, I am conscious of the pain in my chest. I feel as if a boulder is crushing my heart. It stops me from breathing, makes me gasp with pain. Like a wounded beast, I await my fate. I listen for approaching movement. In panic I wait as the seconds drag by. Why does he not come?

Eventually I draw air into my tremulous lungs. It occurs to me that I should move. Perhaps I can recover my gun. It must have fallen close by. Even if I am badly wounded, with a gun I can put up some resistance. I am trapped in this crevice, yet it has provided me with cover.

Tentatively I probe my chest, feeling, I am certain, the stickiness of blood. Yet when I inspect my fingers, there is no redness, only the moistness of sweat. It is not a bullet that struck me, but a sliver of rock, splintered off by an inaccurate shot. I breathe a relieved sigh. I am not dying, at least not yet.

All at once there is movement in the rocks high to my left – a scurrying that gradually recedes into nothingness. It would appear that my assailant has retreated, or is it a ruse?

I flex my limbs. My head feels as if it has been crushed by a squatting buffalo. I explore it with my hand, feel a bump. I wipe the sweat from my eye. I can see the carbine lying just a few yards to my left. Casting caution aside, I scramble across to it, grab hold of it. The mechanism appears undamaged. It is a sturdy weapon.

I gingerly raise my head from the crevice. Surely my enemy has not run off? Perhaps he believes that I am dead, that his shot finished me. Whatever his motive, I must go after him. Either I will kill him, or he will kill me. Once again I pray that my assailant is Buller himself, although I cannot imagine that he would have fled so quickly. My head still hurts but the pain in my chest is receding. Presently, when I feel it with my fingers, I conclude it is just bruising. Whatever injury I have suffered, it has not quelled my determination. And I still have the advantage of knowing the maze of paths, caves and hiding places that exist in this place.

Taking advantage of every shadow, every concealing rock-wall, I search through the Stronghold, my finger curled inside the carbine's trigger-guard. But the morning drifts on, the rain has stopped, a pale sun has even pushed through the cloud. Of course my enemy may be secreted in the gloomy depths of one of the caves, I have no way of telling but to venture into these could be to invite death. I dare not risk it.

At one spot, I hunker down to rest. I open

up my shirt, see the great expanding bruise on my chest. I have experienced yet another amazing escape. Kumookumts is still my ally. How long will he be at my side?

Finally I reach the rocky ramparts. It was from here, some seven months ago, that we Modocs fired down upon the bluecoats.

Again I wipe the sweat from my eye. Once I had been fortunate to possess two eyes. If only I had realized the danger when I was chipping away at that obsidian arrowhead, I would have taken much greater care. However I have no power to alter the past and so I must make do with my single means of vision. And now, thankfully, it serves me well.

About half a mile away, scrambling across away the rocks, I spot a retreating figure. At this distance, I cannot determine whether it is Buller or not. One thing is certain: whoever he is he deserves retribution, not only for my own injury, but for the murders of the Emersons.

I doubt that my quarry knows who I am. I hope that he believes that he killed me back on the rocks, for reasons known only to himself choosing to make a rapid escape. It is in my interest for him to imagine that I'm dead. I leave the Stronghold's ramparts and descend into the ravine-split malpais of the lava beds, treading carefully so as not to turn my ankles. The air is crisp and cold, yet I can feel sweat trickling down beneath my shirt.

The man I stalk appears to be heading for the distant ridge, Gillem's Ridge, where the bluecoats camp had been seven months ago. It would prove a steep climb for him. I must try to catch him before he reaches the top and disappears into the country beyond. I move quickly ignoring the sharpness of the rocks. I have suffered so much physical pain that some more makes little difference. My main concern is to remain hidden from view should he glance back. There is still no way of telling if this man is Buller, nor will there be until I get closer. I try to increase my pace, striving to keep the carbine from clinking against the rocks.

The sky still shows pale blue. I reckon it

must be about noon. I concentrate on the lone figure ahead of me. The distance between us is lessening. Sometimes he disappears as he clambers across a crevice, but before long he reappears and continues his progress. If he knows I am stalking him, he shows no indication. He seems to be a bulky, large man, yet still I cannot determine if he is Buller. Whoever he is, he seems to possess considerable energy as he scrambles onward. I wish he was within gunshot range, but I know my bullet would fall far short.

Suddenly my fortunes change. My familiarity with this cruel terrain does not prevent me from slipping on a treacherous slope. I fall six feet into a crevice, catching my knee on a craggy chunk of rock. I groan with anguish, cursing my stupidity. For a time I can do nothing but sprawl there and allow the pain to wash over me. Eventually the knowledge that my enemy will be gaining distance rouses me into action. Favouring my injured leg, I scramble up, claw my way from the crevice and gasp with frustration.

He is nowhere in sight; perhaps like me he has fallen into some dip, but as I strain my eye, I see no sign of movement. Nonetheless I limp on.

Finally I realize that he must have reached the edge of the lava flow and surmounted the zigzag paths of Gillem's Ridge, where once the army camp was located. At its base there is even a cemetery where some of the bluecoats are buried.

My patience gives out; I no longer strive to conceal myself, and press on with haste, ignoring my pain. If my enemy pauses, holes up in some hidden spot and takes aim at me, so be it.

It is well into the afternoon by the time I reach the edge of the lava flow, cross the narrow swale, and commence climbing towards the summit of the ridge. The pathways are steep, and my progress hampered by my injured leg. After an hour I reach the crest. From here I get clear view of the surrounding terrain. In the far distance, Peninsula Rock and Horse Mountain stand like watchful sentinels. Three miles away, hidden in a depression, is the Stronghold I so recently quit. The surrounding country is filled with tortured rock, cinder-buttes, sharp peaks and dark craters, broken here and there by occasional junipers. Everywhere ugly black lava is spewed, the outflow of ancient volcanoes. The only movement comes from an occasional bird, though there is little here for them to feed upon. In a secluded spot, a thicket of trees, I rest down, feeling utterly weary and frustrated that my enemy appears to have eluded me.

I examine my knee. My trousers, sodden with blood, have been gashed by the rock and through the gaping hole I can see the rawness of the wound. I untuck my shirt, rip off its tail and fashion a crude bandage. I bind it around the wound, hoping that it'll not turn bad. The thought of losing a leg scares me.

Trusting that my enemy is unaware of my presence, or no longer interested, I close my eyes. I have seldom felt more tired in my life. Before long I am asleep.

CHAPTER SEVEN

I sleep for longer than I intended. I shiver in the cold of evening. The man I have been pursuing is long gone. I must turn my thoughts to other aims, particularly in my own survival. I myself am still a hunted man; by this time there will undoubtedly be a reward on my head, dead or alive. Many people will consider that I deserved to die on the gallows along with Jack and the others. I have to decide where I must head for. There are very few places where a renegade Indian will find sanctuary. At least I am still in the familiar country of my youth.

I know that America is a big country; in it there should surely be enough room for both whites and Indians to live, but the white man wants it all for himself. Beyond America there are great seas and beyond these the world is maybe endless. I was taught this when I attended school at Yainax. But it seems long ago now and so much has happened since. Indians have been made even more hateful by the white man's greed. The Americans are relentless in their lust for gold and land, building towns and encroaching upon country that for centuries was the homeland of the Indians. But who am I to talk? Despite the fact that in mind and thought I am a Modoc, the truth is I was born a white man, but my birth is of little help to me. Nobody will believe me anyway.

Sleep has revived me, although my bruised chest throbs with pain and my injured leg seems to possess a reluctance to walk. I curse my carelessness in falling; henceforth my progress will be much slower than it should be. I now have to give up the prospect of catching Buller, at least for the time being. I must concentrate on my own escape.

A strange possibility comes to me. The Pacific Ocean lies to the West of the United States. It is on the shores is San Francisco. In its harbour is the island of Alcatraz. Strangely now I can see that reaching the ocean, perhaps stowing away on a ship, will carry me across the water to the safety of some distant land. But I know that the distance to the sea is great and the land is populated by white people who will perhaps know of my reputation and will be anxious to claim any reward for my capture or killing. I sit with my head down and allow depression to sweep over me. But presently my mood changes. What better opportunity do I have of surviving and retaining my freedom?

None!

I will travel through the night. I wish I still had the horse, but he is long gone by now, perhaps found himself a new owner or perhaps roaming free in the wild. But now I gather my wits, take my bearings from what is left of the sun and start out westward. I have many miles to travel, and the distance will be made even greater by the fact that I must avoid army posts. Even Indians are no longer staunch allies of their less fortunate brothers, brothers who have remained wild to continue the fight for this land that is their birthright. They will be quite satisfied to hand me over for a reward.

With night coming on, I trudge down the far side of Gillem's Bluff, leaving behind me the ghosts of the bluecoats who died in the conflict. The land is vast and lonely, the night is cold with the stars smudged out by low cloud. I cross over the parallel ridges and the sloping plateau east of the ranch lands belonging to the Van Bremer family. They are Indian-haters and I know I will find no sanctuary with them, so I take care to move like a shadow.

But come dawn, I experience an unpleasant shock. I am about to quit a copse of trees, when I hear the blowing of horses. I immediately drop to the ground, conceal myself in long grass.

A column of twenty, mounted bluecoats is crossing the valley ahead of me. Men and animals look weary. I am sure they have been riding through the night, searching for Buller, his men – and me. I hold my breath, fearful that they may pick up some sign of my presence. They come so close I can see the lather on their horses, the weariness in their faces. I cannot take my freedom for granted. At any moment I could be surprised, shot dead or recaptured. Of the two options, I am not sure which I would choose. I eventually conclude that a quick bullet would be better than a slow choke. But for the moment, at least, it will be neither. After what seems an age, the bluecoats are gone, sound of their progress fades, and I am left with a grim knowledge that danger is forever breathing upon me.

At last I am well clear from the spirit land, and beneath me stretches a meadow, a small section of which has been used to seed potatoes or corn. Now only stubble remains. Nearby stands a cabin. Made of virgin timber, it has small windows and a yard and is nestled up against a barn. A chimney pokes from the roof of the cabin but emits no smoke. The outside walls are thickened with earth to keep out the cold and there is a well.

Maybe I have been alone for too long. I feel the need to establish some sort of human company. I creep forward, and when I am nearing the cabin, a dog starts to bark. I should have foreseen such danger. Dropping down, I see the animal – a big white dog. I slip the knife from my belt.

I do not know why but I feel inquisitive about the cabin; it is as if I am being drawn to it by Fate. I rise and move forward ignoring the dog's yapping. At last it stops, lowers its head, and sniffs at me.

It is then I hear a sound from within the cabin. It is a groaning sound that I have heard many times before – the sound of a woman when she is birthing.

The dog comes forward wagging his tail. He has winsome eyes and floppy ears. When he reaches me, I stroke his head. He licks my fingers, and I smile to myself. If danger threatens it will not be from this animal.

Then the cry sounds again from the cabin, even more desperate.

Despite the day's coldness, the door stands open.

Around the cabin the grass and weeds have grown high; the place is in a run-down state. I step up to the door, peer inside. I enter the cabin, step onto the hard-packed earth floor. I pass through the first room which contains a table and a few chairs, one a rocker. There is a small iron stove in the centre which looks dead.

In the second room, I find the woman lying on a tick mattress. She is uncovered, naked, twisting in pain, her belly a bulging mountain.

I groan.

I cannot leave this woman by herself now. I call out in American. I know that my appearance is wild and will bring little comfort. In fact the shock may hasten the birth.

As she sees me horror stifles her cries and she shrieks some strange-sounding words: '*Boze wszechmogacy!* God in Heaven!'

I feel dumbstruck.

'Don't be scared,' I eventually say.

Her dark eyes are wide, great orbes of fear.

She gasps: '*Ty jestes Indianin!* You'll kill me!'

'No!' I manage, as stunned as she is.

She gives me a nightmare stare, her breath rasping.

Suddenly her voice comes again. 'Who … are … you?' And then she repeats, quietly, accusingly: 'You're Indian!'

'What's your name?' I ask. It is a stupid question but is the best I can manage. She does not answer.

I kneel beside the mattress. She turns her head, as if in looking sideways I will go away. For a moment, I wonder if she is insane, perhaps as crazy as Slolux, but then I guess she isn't. Her hair obscures most of her face. She is glistening with sweat and is grinding her teeth. The cords in her neck stand out. Her feet start kicking spasmodically.

'How long have you been here?' I ask.

At last she responds to me. It is as if she

has decided that she has no option but to trust me. 'One day, one night,' she says. 'Too long.'

She is not American. She must come from some distant land.

'Where is your man?' I ask.

'He go to town for midwife. They be back soon.'

I shake my head in bewilderment. What man would leave a woman in this state for so long?

It seems ages since I last witnessed a birthing at my mother's side. Now this woman's legs are wide apart. She seems stretched to her limit.

She pants, gasps, grunts, bears down. I see the swelling of the baby's head, the wet, dark oval of its hair. She presses her chin against her chest and strains with the massive effort of a woman trying to move a mountain. Her eyes are narrowed to slits, her lips white. She is being tortured by the living creature struggling to escape from her belly.

'Your baby comes … see!' I shout.

The head emerges gradually, face up. The features are wrinkled, the eyes clenched, the skin strangely blue. Then the birth seems to stop, it seems even to retract and I am fearful that the baby will return to the womb. But my fears are unfounded. With new momentum the baby comes partly into the world. I grasp hold of its tiny shoulders, pull it clear like a slippery fish. The woman shrieks, swears at me: '*Gadzino – you snake!*'

It is a girl-child, but she is not breathing.

I turn her upside down, locking one hand around her ankles; with the other I slap her buttocks. Still nothing. I blow in to her tiny nostrils, try to surprise her, then, in desperation, I press my finger and thumb through the tiny slit of her mouth, stretching it wide, gripping her tongue, pulling it back and forth. When I pause, I sigh with relief.

She is breathing … choking, sobbing little breaths.

I have won the battle. My mother would be proud.

'Cut cord,' the new mother gasps. Tears

are streaming down her cheeks. 'Knife's in drawer.'

I use my own knife. Afterward, I fill a bucket with water from the outside well. What I do then is what I watched my mother perform countless times.

Later the woman gazes at me. Somehow she finds the strength to speak, even tries to smile. 'My name is Klara Quaternight. I am Polish.' And then almost impishly she adds: 'Pleased to meet you!'

The situation is crazy. What am I to do? Why is this woman alone? Where is her man? Is he likely to return at any moment, find me and resent my presence? I take the baby back to the woman, place it against her chest. Her breasts are large. The baby makes no attempt to suck. I try to encourage it, to show it what to do, but achieve nothing. It seems all the baby wants to do is rest.

After a while I look around. Alongside the stove is some wood. There are matches upon the table. I shave some wood. I work on the fire, fan the flames and shortly they are ablaze. The dog comes and sits at my side, enjoying the warmth.

Klara Quarternight suddenly comes awake.

'You see,' I say, 'there is no need to be afraid of me.'

'I not afraid of you,' she says. 'I afraid you go away.'

After a moment she asks, 'Who are you?'

'Call me ... Michael.'

'You are Indian.'

'No, I am not Indian. I'm a white man.'

The baby makes a gurgling sound. 'She needs to be fed,' I say.

She holds her to her breast, tries to make her suck. But it is no good. 'The milk will not come,' she says. Her eyes show frustration. Both mother and baby are distressed.

I remember a trick my stepmother used to use. I go to the dog, sitting by the fire. I take his head in my hand. He is puzzled by what I am doing. The baby's cries are growing more intense. I can feel the woman watching me in bewilderment.

'Michael… What you do?'

'This may help you,' I say.

The dog lifts his lip, bares his teeth. He is an old dog. He is as puzzled as the woman. Perhaps he will bite me. But before he can, I check the whiskers sprouting from his muzzle, find the stiffest. I pluck the whisker out and he may have bitten me but I draw back quickly. The whisker is like a needle. I go to the woman and gently probe her nipples with the whisker, trying to open them. They are tender.

'Keep still,' I say.

She is trusting me but her discomfort is evident from her shuddering breath. She is very brave. I work the whisker back and forth on both nipples and presently the watery whiteness of milk seeps out from her left breast. I massage it, drawing out the first milk. Fifteen minutes later the baby sucks contentedly on it but the right nipple remains blocked. Afterwards the little one sleeps contentedly. So does her mother.

It grows warm within the cabin and I keep the fire high. I do not know what I am going to do. It will be dangerous to stay here for long.

The baby begins to gurgle. I take her from the sleeping woman and sit with her in my arms rocking back and forth. She goes quiet. A feeling of contentment settles over me.

Later the fire emits a loud crackle I am startled to wakefulness. I fear the woman's husband has returned, but when I see that nothing is changed I doze again. At last the morning comes and cold grey light seeps through the windows.

Klara Quarternight is awake. For the first time I notice that her eyes are green, like spring grass, although when in deep shadow they appear as black as her hair. She has a habit of flicking her head to one side to clear the hair from her face. Her gaze becomes fixed on me. I squirm uneasily.

'I am grateful,' she says.

CHAPTER EIGHT

I have taken refuge in the cabin. I don't know how long I can stay here, nor how safe I am. If Mr Quarternight returns, I don't know what will happen. Throughout the day one thing becomes increasingly clear. Although the baby is thriving, her mother is not. Despite her courage, it is clear she is in great pain. I have been unable to unblock her right breast. It has become swollen like a hard grapefruit. It is a problem beyond my powers to cure. She must have further assistance as soon as possible, and if I leave her I will have behaved even worse than her wayward husband.

Her pain increases. She smiles bravely, says she will be all right but I know that is not true. I'm afraid she could die.

I keep the fire roaring and ensure she and

the little one are well wrapped with blankets. With great effort she eventually gets up from her bed, gingerly washes herself in the water I have warmed, and dresses. She moves about totteringly, attending to minor chores, mainly to take her mind off the pain. But there are times when she is so unsteady that I need to support her.

I think Klara Quarternight is the same age as me. And she is an inquisitive person.

To distract her from her suffering I try to get her talking. I cannot explain, but there is something about her that I find captivating. I think it is her courage or perhaps the greenness of her eyes.

'Michael,' she says, 'you come from heaven. You are an angel.'

I smile. 'There are many who disagree. They think I am a devil!'

'Then you are an angelic devil!'

She sits in a rocking chair, close to the fire, the baby in her arms.

'What will you call her?' I ask.

'Agata. That was my mother's name.'

I feel certain Klara will not betray me.

I find some wood in the barn, and during the second day I fashion a cradle for Agata.

In the evening when we are sitting warmly beside the stove, Agata at Klara's breast, I make up my mind. Her right nipple is still blocked, the pain terrible. She cannot go on like this. She must be taken to a doctor and I know that the nearest doctor is at Yreka. I also know that going near the town will place me in the greatest jeopardy. But in my mind, all else seems to fade into insignificance when compared with her suffering. I have never felt this way towards a woman before.

To occupy her thoughts, I confide in her, telling her that although I was brought up by the Indians, I was born a white man. She knows well enough of the troubles that arose between the soldiers and the Modocs, but she holds no hatred for the Indians, having always found them friendly. When I tell her about the fate of the Emerson family, tears spring to her cheeks. She cups her face in her hands, shuddering with grief.

Still deeply shaken, she later listens gravely as I relate my own story. I tell her about my reprieve from the gallows and her green eyes widen with compassion.

'Poor Michael,' she says and then repeats it: 'Poor Michael. It reminds me of my own dear family.' She gives me a quick glance. 'My mother was raped and murdered by the Russians. My father was sent to Siberia where he died. You have heard about the troubles between Poland and Russia?'

Somewhat ashamed, I shake my head.

'Well, to get away from trouble my sister and me come to New York. But things were difficult for us. Then we heard that men in the West wanted wives. We advertized our names in a catalogue and travelled to San Francisco. I met Henry Quarternight. I thought him a good, kind man, so I said yes, I would marry him. But it was big mistake. He wasn't like he seemed.' She dragged a trembling hand across her brow. 'The drink, the gambling, the other women...'

We sit for a long while thinking about what we discussed. Every so often she winces as a spasm of pain catches her.

But presently, in her still weak voice, she poses a candid question: 'Michael, did you help murder General Canby?'

I hang my head. The fact is I did not shoot Canby, but nor did I strive to prevent it. I was as foolish as most of the Modocs in believing that if the general was killed, the bluecoats would go away. I should have known that white people do not reason this way, that they will lust for revenge just as fiercely as any Indian.

'Captain Jack did not want to hurt General Canby,' I told her. 'But Hooker Jim accused him of being a coward, and some of the other people said that unless he killed Canby he was no longer worthy of being chief. Jack was a proud man and this hurt him.'

I pause, wondering if my story is tiring her, but she is hanging on my every word.

'Jack came to me and asked if I would help

him,' I continue. 'The arrangement for the powwow was that neither side should carry guns, but nobody believed that this promise would be kept. Jack asked me if, at the time he met Canby and the other peace commissioners, I and Slolux would hide in a nearby ravine with several guns available in case they were needed. I had always respected Jack. I would have done anything for him.'

'Go on,' she prompts.

'I did not believe the shooting would happen. I believed that Jack and Canby would make some arrangement for peace, that the bluecoats would allow us to stay in the Stronghold provided there was no more trouble.'

Her face shows concern, as if she is sharing my turmoil. 'What happened?' she asks.

It is a long time since I've spoken at such length. I clear my throat, then go on. 'Hooker Jim and the others taunted the peace commissioners. I could hear everything they said from where I was hidden. And suddenly voices were raised and things had gone too far. There was no turning back. Almost immediately guns started firing and Slolux and I rose to our feet so as to take more guns to Jack.'

Klara Quarternight is shaking her dark head, dismayed.

'Showing ourselves,' I continue, 'was a big mistake. Bluecoats on the bluff had a magic glass which made everything seem close. They saw what happened and they saw everybody who was there. They believe we were all guilty of the murder, although the truth is I would never have hurt Canby. I believe he was a good man who wanted to help us. Afterwards, Jack said his bullets slipped, which was the Modoc way of saying he was sorry about the murder. It was weeks later that we surrendered. The bluecoats promised us that we would not be harmed if we gave up, but they broke their word. We were put on trial, six of us who'd been at the powwow. They told us we would all hang. But at the final moment the Grandfather in

Washington sent a message. Slolux and me were not to die.'

'*Listen!*' In her weakened state it is a great effort for her to call out.

It is the next morning. I immediately stop placing wood in the stove. I hold my breath and realize why she is alarmed. We hear the stomp of horses, the creak of harness from outside. I quell my panic. She lifts the curtain, peers through the window. 'Bluecoats. You must hide - quick!'

I glance around the room in desperation, seeing only chairs and a table. 'Where?'

Approaching horses sound very close.

'The cellar!' she cries. 'Hurry, God's sake!'

She points to the small trap door in the centre of the floor and I scramble across to it. My heart is pounding like a hammer. I hook my fingers into the trap-door's metal ring and to my relief the hinged door lifts to reveal the dark pit beneath. The opening is small, but I drop through it, landing on the heap of vegetables that cover the floor.

Straight away Klara has replaced the trap door and I'm plunged into darkness.

I struggle to calm myself. The air is stifling, thick with the smell of vegetables, but I force myself to breathe steadily. I remain perfectly still. I can hear Klara moving around above me and also the gentle murmurings of baby Agata. But now other sounds intrude: the voices of men. Clearly, the column of blue-coats has halted outside the front of the cabin.

'Hi there! Anybody at home!' a call sounds.

Slowly Klara moves to the door and opens it. A man's voice says: 'I'm Sergeant Buckhurst. We're from Fort Klamath. We are looking for what's left of the outlaws who shot a military escort. They also murdered the Emerson family. We tracked down some of them, ambushed them near Peninsular Point. Killed their leader, a brute called Buller.'

Blood is pounding in my head. Buller is dead! May his soul rot in hell! He and his murderers deserve nothing less.

'But there's still an Indian roaming free,' the sergeant continues. 'He's as dangerous as hell, maybe worse than Buller. They call him the Modoc Kid. For heaven's sake, keep your eyes open and make sure your door stays bolted. You're mighty vulnerable here. Crazy living in a place like this. Still, I guess that's your business.'

I hear the creak of saddle leather. 'You look downright poorly. Is your husband around?'

'He go to town,' Klara explains, her voice trembling. 'Him fetch the doctor. He'll be back soon. I just had a baby.'

I hear the sound of footsteps above me; with horror I realize that the sergeant has entered the cabin. I imagine his eyes probing all around. I pray there is nothing to show I have been here. At least Klara can blame anything on her husband.

'My men need to fill their canteens,' the sergeant is saying. He has a brisk, impatient way of speaking. I decide he is not a man to be crossed. I do not remember him from Fort Klamath, but guess that additional bluecoats have been brought in to hunt down those responsible for the violence. With Buller dead, they have done good work. If the blue-coats knew that I had killed two more of the outlaws, maybe they would not hate me so much.

Klara says: 'Your men – please to help themselves from the well.'

I realize with dismay that the Sergeant is standing upon the trap-door of the cellar, his weight making it creak. I am sure he is a heavy man and am scared that he will crash through on top of me. To worsen matters, he stamps his foot.

'Ah,' he says, 'you have a cellar.'

'For vegetables.' Klara responds.

'Maybe somebody is hiding down there,' he says suspiciously. 'I best check.'

Klara's voice comes impatiently: 'No-body's there. I should know.'

And then she adds something that makes my blood freeze: 'If you think I lie, look for yourself!'

I am aware that he steps aside. I hear his

scornful laugh. 'That won't be necessary.'

Very quietly I start breathing again.

Crouching like a rabbit in its burrow, I allow time to drag away. I believe other blue-coats enter the cabin, warming themselves by the fire. One of them says: 'I hope your man comes back soon. It ain't right a woman being alone in a place like this, not with a dangerous Injun roaming around and you having just had a babe. You look as if you need that doctor real bad.'

'We best send a doctor over from Fort Klamath,' another man says.

'No!' Klara responds. 'No need for that.'

It seems a lifetime, maybe longer, before the bluecoats leave. It is probably less than ten minutes. I am stiff with cramp. After they have gone Klara opens the trap door, allowing light to flood in. Clumsily, I straighten up, climb from the hole. She looks deathly pale. I guess she has suffered as badly as I have, but she has acted bravely.

'Thank God they go,' she says.

I glance at her, still astonished at her

action. 'Why did you tell him to look in the cellar?'

Almost collapsing, she sits heavily down on a chair, drained by events. 'I knew he would not do anything I suggested,' she said. 'Some men will never do what woman suggests.' She buries her face in her hands.

I can't help it. I laugh. She is an incredible woman. Minutes later she is feeding the baby.

'Why hasn't your husband come home?' I ask.

'Something bad must have happened,' she says.

'Has he let you down before, in other ways, I mean?'

CHAPTER NINE

She looks perplexed, as if trying to think good of him yet unable to do so. At last she stops trying: 'Henry not a reliable man. He said if I marry him everything would be wonderful, that the government here wanted people to come to Oregon, almost giving land away to those who would work hard.'

She frowns. Her memories are sad.

'What I not understand, was that he had weaknesses. He always want to drink; he gambled like crazy and there were the other women. My sister fell in love with a good man and they married. Henry drank too much at the wedding, made a fool of himself. We bought this land, but he was lazy, didn't work it properly. He say I nag too much.'

I can see she is growing tired. 'Tell me the rest tomorrow,' I say.

During the night things get bad. She does not sleep and tosses restlessly on the bed; frantic with pain.

I press a cold compress against her, but it brings little relief. Her breast remains hard and swollen.

'I must take you into the doctor at Yreka,' I say.

'No,' she argues. 'It's too dangerous for you.'

'It will be dangerous for you, and the baby, if you don't see a doctor.'

She is too weak to argue but her face is creased with concern.

I try to get her to take some food next morning but she cannot.

'Maybe you can take me to Yreka and drop me near the doctor's house. Then you can leave before anybody realizes who you are.'

'We'll see.'

As the sun rises, I step outside. The surrounding country appears quiet. I collect the harness from the barn and then go to the meadow where a placid grey horse is grazing. Soon I have the harness upon him, lead him back to the barn and get him within the shanks of the wagon. After this, I return to the cabin. Klara has managed to dress, though she is very tottery upon her feet. Her face is ashen but even so it occurs to me that she is a good-looking woman and deserves a better life than that of living in this place. This gives me a strange feeling. For so many years white women have meant nothing to me. Now this woman makes me realize I have white blood in my veins.

Why on earth has her husband deserted her in this way! He has now been gone almost a week, seeming not to care that she was in such distress. Did the birth of his baby mean so little to him?

I ask myself why I care. What difference does it make to me whether this woman or her child survive? And yet for some reason I *do* care.

The day is cold, the sky is dull-grey. Perhaps it will not be too long before snow or sleet begins to fall. The baby, Agata, is wrapped in a warm blanket, her little face gazing out with unfocused eyes. I know that in going to Yreka, I am taking the gravest risk, yet instinct tells me that if I do not get Klara to a doctor she will worsen and die.

I lay a mattress in the wagon and help her onto it. I cover her and the baby with another blanket, and then I climb onto the wagon's seat and set the horse in motion. I know the way to Yreka. It is a town that has flourished because of the rich harvesting of gold from surrounding streams. Along with Jack I visited it many times in bygone years, even helped to put out a fire at a bakery. I know there is a doctor there. I pray he will be an expert in woman's matters. I know if Klara had lived with us in the village on the Lost River, the midwives and shamans would have gone to work and done what was necessary to cure her. I wish my own knowledge was deep enough to do what was necessary. It is not, but at least I saved the child from dying at birth.

And so we set out along the rough trail and I try to avoid the ruts as much as possible. She will undoubtedly be even weaker by the time we reach town. I wonder if, when we arrive, we will find out what happened to her husband. Perhaps he has met with some accident or been murdered. Perhaps he is not even in town. Several times Klara murmured his name 'Henry ... where are you? Why don't you come?'

I have no answer. I just pull my hat low over my face and concentrate on urging the old horse onward. Several times we pass wagons going the other way. Sometimes their occupants call out, but all I do is wave. I dare not get too close in case my face and reputation have become known. Every hour or so we stop and I try to get Klara to take a little of the food and drink some water. There is no talk between us; she is too weak for words. She breastfeeds the baby and I am thankful that she has at least one functioning tit.

As we travel we pass more cabins, ranch houses and small-holdings. I am fearful that somebody may come out to greet us, to show us hospitality and in so doing realize that this woman is in the company of the murderous 'Modoc Kid'. Soon we are entering the town with its criss-cross of streets, brick built buildings, banks and church.

On this cold day, with sleet driving into our faces, Main Street is deserted. Klara knows the town, knows where the doctor lives. She directs me to it and we draw up outside. I tremble. If anybody recognizes me, I am be done for. Yet for the moment I can not turn tail, leave this woman.

With hat-brim pulled down and coat-collar drawn high, I climb from the wagon and ring the bell to the doctor's surgery. There is a long pause, then the door is opened and a plump woman appears, her face wincing as the cold wind catches her.

I try to speak in my best English, hoping she will not recognize me as an Indian.

'Dr Elliott?' I say. 'Is he here? I have a woman with me. She has given birth. She is in great pain.'

The woman's expression changes to one of concern. 'Bring her inside,' she says. 'I'll get my husband straight away.'

Klara clutches baby Agata tightly. I help them from the wagon. Together we enter the house and the warmth of the place rises to meet us like a welcoming dog. Within minutes, the white-haired Dr Elliott appears and, seeing how weak Klara is, motions her to rest down upon the sofa. He quickly examines her, and then motions to his wife to take her into another room.

'Her breast,' he says to his wife. 'The milk duct is badly blocked. You know what you must do.'

His wife nods, and as she assists Klara and Agata into the next room, Klara calls to me: 'Michael, I'm so grateful for all you have done.'

Dr Elliott turns to me. 'My wife will free the duct,' he says. 'She has helped many women in this way. She'll be all right, but she will need rest for a few days. She must stay here.'

What I do not realize is that he knows Klara and, more importantly, he knows her husband and where he is.

'Come back later,' he says. 'I cannot promise that this lady will have recovered. As I say, she needs rest and medicine.'

I nod and back from the room. A moment later I am standing on the sidewalk near the wagon and the patiently waiting horse. The options that are open to me fill my mind. I can climb onto the wagon, leave town and seek obscurity in the hills and forests, believing that Klara and her child are in the best possible hands. I can return to the life of a wild animal which allowed me a degree of freedom. If I linger in this place, sooner or later my identity will be discovered and I will be thrown in jail to await anything that fate has in store. But Klara may still need me, especially now that her husband seems to have disappeared.

However as I wrestle with my uncertainty, the door of the doctor's house opens and a young boy comes out and rushes down the street, not sparing me a glance. Yet something about his urgency warns me that his mission is connected to me. I climb up onto the wagon's seat, flick the reins, and set the horse in motion. Moving quite slowly, having little idea of where I am heading, I am suddenly aware of the boy again. This time there is a man accompanying him. He is a small man, and as he goes past he glances in my direction and there is something strange about his expression. Somehow I know that this man is Klara's husband – Henry Quarternight.

I set the wagon onward, and at last I reach the outskirts of town where I stop. If my conclusion is correct, this individual seems totally unworthy of being the husband of Klara. I know her to be a sweet and brave woman. What a worthless soul he was to desert her in her hour of need. Had Kumookumts not guided my footsteps to their cabin, her fate would have been terrible. My escape has enabled me to save lives as well as destroy them.

I find shelter beneath some tall trees, thankful that I am out of the driving seat. I wait, yet I do not know what I am waiting for. Perhaps some guidance will come from Kumookumts. Perhaps his messenger will come down from the heavens and tell me what I should do, where I should go. No messenger comes and I do not know why I took my next action. For some crazy reason, I turn the wagon around and drive back the way I have come, halting once again outside Dr Elliott's surgery. With uncertainty slowing my movements, I ring the bell and am shortly greeted again by Mrs Elliott.

'She's going to be all right,' she announces, 'The milk is flowing, her husband is here and the baby's fine. But the lady is asking for you. You are Michael?'

I nod.

'Then you must come in. I think her husband wants to speak with you, to thank you for what you have done.'

Her words bring me no comfort but I follow her inside and the door closes behind

126

me and I feel, quite suddenly, that I may well have walked into a trap.

I do not see Klara. I imagine that she has been put to bed for rest. But as Mrs Elliott leads me into her parlour, I am unpleasantly surprised by the presence of the man I saw earlier in the street.

The doctor's wife provides the introductions. 'This is Henry Quarternight,' she said and then nodding in my direction she adds, 'and this is the gentleman who brought your wife and baby in. Had it not been for him, God knows what would have happened.'

I feel shocked. This is the first time that anybody has called me a 'gentleman'.

Henry Quarternight is a furtive man, some years older than his wife. There is something shifty about him. His eyes are shining as if he is over-excited. But nonetheless he smiles broadly and reaches out with his hand. We shake. His gaze remains on my face for what seems overlong. I am desperate to ask the question: where were you when your wife needed you so badly? But I hold my tongue and he speaks first.

'I'm real grateful for what you did. Klara has told me that without you she would have died – and the baby too. It is an honour to shake your hand.'

I nod. I am aware that my appearance is still very much Indian.

'Are you hungry?' Mrs Elliott asks.

'Yes,' I manage, wondering if she is aware of the rumble in my stomach.

'Then I will get you some food and leave you two together. I am sure you have plenty to discuss. Take your coat off, Michael. Make yourself at home by the fire.'

I do as instructed, remove my coat and am immediately aware of the ragged state of my clothing which I have not changed since my escape. If Henry Quarternight is puzzled by my appearance he does not show it. There is a heartiness and friendliness about him that leaves me feeling uneasy. We sit on chairs, warming ourselves by the fire which had been piled high with logs. I cannot remember the last time I was in such a room.

CHAPTER TEN

He glances around the room as if to make certain we are not overheard. From elsewhere in the house comes the rattling of pots and I guess that Mrs Elliott is preparing the meal, but from within the room the only sound is the crackle of the fire. The thought of food makes my mouth water.

'Of course this is man-to-man,' Quarternight starts out, giving me a wink. 'Everything went mighty wrong. When Klara started showing signs she was about to produce she said I should go and get the midwife. To tell the truth, I wasn't too keen on hanging around while she gave birth. To my mind that's woman's business. I'm sure you agree. So I was glad enough to set off for town to let the midwife know what was happening.'

He is speaking slowly, as if confessing events is a great strain. What I should realize is that he has other reasons for taking his time.

'When I arrived in town, I went straight to the midwife's, but she wasn't there. I spoke to a Spanish servant girl who didn't know much English, but I thought she understood what was happening. She said the midwife should be back in a couple of hours as she was helping some other wretched woman. Anyway, I scribbled out a note asking the midwife to go out to my cabin as quick as she could.'

He lifts up the poker from the hearth, gives the logs a poke, sending a shower of sparks up the chimney.

'I been riding hard to get to town, worked up a thirst, so I guessed a little time in the saloon wouldn't do no harm. I had a couple of beers and a bite to eat, and then one of the girls got talking to me and I told her what was happening and she was, well, kind of understanding. She said maybe I should rest and she said I could use her room upstairs. So I said okay and sure enough her room was right comfy, and her bed was really inviting. She said I could take my time as the midwife would make sure Klara was all right. It was woman's business and men were best out the way. You know what saloon females are like I'm sure.' He puts on a sheepish expression.

He glances out the window, down the street. It is as if he is expecting something. Nonetheless he turns his attention back to me. 'She said I could stay at her place as long as I wanted. She brought me some more whisky. I ended up staying the night, and then a couple more. I felt pretty sure Klara would be all right, so what had I to worry about?' He shrugged and gave another one of his wry smiles. 'When a female is about to produce, she turns mean, holds back on giving her man his rights. Mind you, I never guessed the midwife didn't get my message. It was a good job you came along. That's why I'm so grateful. Kind of restored my faith in human nature.'

It is now that I finally decide that something queer is going on. I also decide it is time to get out – fast. I stand up, pull on my coat. 'I got to go,' I say. 'Some urgent business.'

His manner changes immediately. The smile is gone and suddenly he has drawn the pistol from his holster and is pointing it at me. His voice now comes as a snarl.

'Too true you've got urgent business. I know who you are, you filthy Indian. You're as guilty as sin, murdering honest white folk, and you ain't playing about with my wife no more. Lucky you didn't murder her as well.'

I feel as if the blood has drained from my veins. His words seem to echo round within my head. Foolishly, I have left my own weapon leaning against the wall at the side of the room. All I have within reach is my knife and for a second I consider drawing it and throwing myself upon him regardless of whether or not he could get a bullet into me, but any such action is interrupted by the urgent ringing of the outside bell. All at once I am aware of the heavy clump of boots, of a man's voice, and then the door to the room bursts open and two bulky men shoulder their way in. Both are brandishing guns; both have silver badges pinned to their coats.

'It's him all right!' Quaternight shouts. With his left hand he reaches into his pocket and draws out a paper, practically ramming it into my face. It is a "wanted notice", bearing an unmistakable picture of my face which looks as ugly as sin. 'The Modoc Kid,' he spits at me. 'You should be strung up straight away, like you should have been in the first place.'

'Now hold on,' the lawman who is obviously Town Marshal says. His face resembles a crumpled blanket. 'You're right. This is the Modoc Kid, no doubt whatsoever. But this is a law-abiding community and he'll face justice the same way as any other killer. The judge will make sure that he

133

gets his just deserts.'

His deputy has taken possession of my carbine, is emptying the chamber of shells.

I stand there, knowing that I have no way out. Mrs Elliott has re-entered the room, her amazed eyes taking in the scene. 'I guess you won't have time to eat,' she says, her expression reflecting disappointment.

I know that my disappointment is worse than hers. I am gutted, plunged into a deep hole of despair. My throat seems constricted, as if fingers are trying to choke me.

The deputy's lips are so mean-thin they are invisible. He is pointing his pistol directly at me and he is so close that any slight pressure from his trigger finger will blast me into the next world. I have little alternative but to swallow back the fury boiling inside me and hold out my hands as ordered. Within a second handcuffs link my wrists, and my period of freedom is over.

I have been a fool. I should have realized that Quarternight was no more genuine than a rattlesnake. Although what he told me about how he deserted his wife in her hour of need may have been true, he dragged out the time to allow news of my presence to be passed to the marshal. Perhaps wanted notices were posted far and wide, and he is seeing an opportunity to not only arrange the capture of me, but also to collect the reward that was on offer. He is a greedy and wicked man. Nobody would turn to drink and a cheap woman's body when his wife is in dire need.

But now it is too late for regrets. Within five minutes, I am outside in the bitter cold once more, the wind driving sleet into me. I am frogmarched between the marshal and his deputy down the street. We are soon inside the jail and I am shoved into a cell, the door slammed shut, the key turned. I drop onto the wooden bunk, my one eye blurred with tears of bitter frustration.

There are no other prisoners in jail, and I am left alone to brood on my misfortune for what seems hours. How I long for the freedom of the mountains and the trees and the lakes, but now I am trapped again as surely as any bird in a cage. The only comfort I receive comes in the form of fresh clothing – canvas jacket, linen shirt, jeans and a pair of old boots. I am glad of these because my old ones had been reduced to shreds.

That evening Marshal Frazer formally charges me with escaping from the military, and in so doing murdering several soldiers.

In addition he charges me with the killing of the Emerson family. He says that the coat I am wearing belonged to Mr Emerson, providing further evidence of my guilt.

'You will stand trial before Judge Smith,' he told me. 'You will get fair justice, but I don't think you should hold out too much hope for your future. Like most people think, you should have been hanged with the rest of those Modocs at Fort Klamath. That would have saved a few innocent white lives.'

I don't respond. Later I learn that my trial will be held in two or three weeks' time.

Meanwhile there is evidence to be collected.

When I am once more left alone, I can rant and rave, fight the iron bars of my cell, but of course such action will gain me nothing. So I withdraw into my inner self, steeped in my misery. I try to see into the future, try to find some glimmer of hope. It seems I have no friends left in the world, nobody who will give me any support. A succession of deputies take their turn in the office, guarding me. From their conversation, I gather that there is much anger in the town, a burning desire to see justice administered more quickly than that which is provided through the courts of law. I even hear men shouting from the outside street, calling that I be handed over to them so that they can carry out retribution. The Emerson family was popular in town, friends to all, and their brutal murders has aroused seething fury. And I now know, without doubt, that I am the target for their hatred. They want me dead, choked at the end of the rope, but now, strangely, it is the law that is

137

protecting me, albeit for only the brief period before I stand before Judge Smith and my fate will be in the hands of a jury who are craving for my death.

Over the next days in that cell, the scraps of food I am given leave me feeling starved. The only warmth comes from a stove in the main office, but this is minimal and I am allowed the thinnest of blankets to wrap around myself. I feel frozen and the drafts cut through my cell like a bitter blizzard. I long for the warmth of a wickiup, for the companionship of my old Indian friends. I have spent many days in the wilderness, yet in this place I feel the cold more than ever, and it has a cough irritating my chest.

Within a few weeks my life may be over; now I feel no inclination to argue my innocence.

There was little communication between me and the men who guard me, apart from when Marshal Frazer questions me. His words are angled in such a way as to increase the impression of my guilt. I retreat behind the simpleton's façade which, perhaps, saved my life at Fort Klamath.

Meanwhile I comply with every order given, washing in a bucket of cold water, emptying my slop pail, cleaning the dishes on which my meagre food is served.

The hours pass, became days that slowly drag into weeks. My brain becomes numbed. I give up trying to consider possibilities. Where fear, perhaps panic, should be there was nothing apart from the longing I feel to be with Klara again. How is that cruel man treating her?

There are always two or three guards on duty in the marshal's office, and there is but a small outside window to my cell. Escape is impossible and I have to resign myself to my fate.

During the final week before my trial, a young man visits me. His name is Kirby, tall and skinny as a spider. He constantly chews at his fingernails. He tells me that he has come to help me and that he is a lawyer. After a lengthy bite at his fingernail, he carefully studies the notes that Marshal Frazer has made, asking more questions and scribbling away. He has honest eyes and seems to have a genuine wish to help me. I relate the truth of events to him and he appears to believe me. I feel a compulsion to trust him, that he may offer me my only hope.

One joy brightens my days. Klara visits me. She has made a wonderful recovery, is resplendent in the bloom of motherhood. For a moment I am speechless in admiration. She is truly beautiful – but her face is clouded with sadness, her eyes brimming with tears.

'Had it not been for me,' she says, 'you would still be free, Michael. I feel so guilty.'

She is suddenly in my arms, hugging me tightly, not in passion but in something beyond that. All I can say is that she is very special to me in a way I have never known before. For a moment all that seems to matter is that she has recovered; all else is forgotten. She says that her husband is taking her home that afternoon, that he has promised to mend his ways. But she will never forgive him for betraying me. All too soon she is forced to depart; our hands remain linked for a moment, then slip reluctantly apart.

The final days speed along and early one morning Marshal Frazer unlocks my cell and tells me to prepare myself for trial. He is his usual grim-faced and unfriendly self and he makes doubly sure that my handcuffs are secure before I am led out from my cell and down the street to a grand new building which is the courthouse.

'Judge Smith has all the evidence he needs to convict you,' he tells me.

CHAPTER ELEVEN

I am now in the hands of fate. I can feel the hatred that exists amongst the townsfolk of Yreka. It scorches me. There must be at least fifty people present as I am led into the courtroom. The judge himself, Edward Smith, is seated on a platform. His face is hard, his nose large and his chin like a lump of granite. His expression is as severe as those of the rest of the gathering and when his voice comes it reminds me of a sharp knife, slicing out words. The trial at Fort Klamath was conducted under military arrangements. Today I am to be tried by a judge and jury which is now the civilian practice. I doubt that the last-minute mercy the army granted me will be repeated.

My mind remains numb as proceedings commence. I sit between two guards, linked to them by handcuffs, and watch as lawyers and witnesses are sworn in.

The formal charges are made: escape and murder of guards; the rape and killing of the Emerson family. I plead not guilty.

The first witness stands up, and under intense questioning, relates how he had come upon the Emerson homestead and found their mutilated bodies. He also tells how Mr Emerson had been scalped Indian-fashion. Again, accusing eyes swing in my direction and voices murmur angrily.

'The Modoc Kid is a killer and rapist,' the prosecuting attorney shouts. A big, heavily moustached man, he stands hands on hips. 'The Modoc Kid was even wearing the coat of poor Mr Emerson, snatched from his home shortly after he was choked to death. This Indian also carried out unmentionable atrocities on Mrs Emerson and her children.

There can be no doubt about his guilt, and I maintain that he deserves nothing less than the severest penalty.'

There are shouts of agreement from the gathered assembly. My legs feel weak. I doubt I could stand up even if I am ordered to do so.

The defence counsel, the young lawyer called Kirby, now comes to his feet. He bites his thumb nail, then speaks in a steady voice. He relates the truth as I told it to him, despite the many times members of the assembly interrupt, shouting their abuse so loudly that the judge is obliged to bang his hammer.

Kirby continues undeterred. 'This Indian was the victim of unfortunate circumstance,' he proclaims. 'He had no part in contriving the massacre of the army escort. This was the work of Buller's gang. It was only by a twist of fate that Barncho managed to escape. I put it to you: any normal person would have done the same. He did not kill any soldiers or attempt to harm them. That was the work of Buller's outlaws. Thankfully, most of these brigands have since paid the penalty, being hunted down and destroyed

144

by the army. Buller himself is now in his grave, together with some of those who took part in the atrocity against the Emerson family.'

He pauses, allowing his words to sink in. Judge Smith is holding his head to one side, listening intently. Kirby clears his throat and then continues.

'Barncho has told me how, after seeing for himself the bodies of the Emersons and borrowing the coat of Mr Emerson, he trailed the criminals. He eventually found that the outlaw party had split up, but he chose to follow the group that was heading for the Lava Beds. Here, he killed two of the murderers and would have done the same to the third had he been able. A party of settlers has now recovered the bodies of the two dead men from the Modoc Stronghold and they currently reside in the town mortuary. After inflicting this just punishment, he came across a cabin and found a woman who was in the process of giving birth. He was immensely helpful to her, saving both her life and that of her baby.'

At this there are shouts of disbelief in the courtroom. How can a savage Indian, a killer, show such mercy to a white woman?

I look at the jury – eight stonefaced townsmen, but they avoid my gaze. I guess that they, like everybody else, cannot believe this story. It seems too preposterous for any white man to accept, for they generally believe that no Indian has a glimmer of kindness or compassion in his soul.

But there is a surprise in store for everybody, including myself. A pale faced Klara enters the court room and is sworn in. To me, at this moment, no vision of female beauty can be more perfect. When called upon to do so, she speaks up in a strong voice.

'I owe this man Barncho my life,' she says, her green eyes flashing defiantly. 'If he not arrive when he did, I would surely be dead. I know he is not capable of the murder he is accused of. He is a kind man. I swear that before God.' Her final words of, 'He must be acquitted!' are drowned out by the uproar in the courtroom. As she steps down from the stand, she glances in my direction and smiles, and that smile is like a shaft of sunshine lifting my spirits.

My lawyer Kirby has another trick up his sleeve for a further witness is called. He is wearing a fine plumed hat and full military uniform which displays three chevrons. He supports himself on crutches. He wears an eye-shield and his face bears horrible scars. This is the man I gave water to after the massacre of the escort. I imagined him dead, but clearly he was rejected by the spirit world, though his condition still remains poorly. Even so he responds to Kirby's promptings with assurance.

'This Indian took no part in the killing of my bluecoats. He gave me water when I needed it, tried to help me, only ran off when he knew that other men had arrived who would see to me.'

Having spoken, he appears overcome by his weakness, needs immediate support. When he leaves the court I feel towards him

147

a tremendous surge of gratitude.

Both the prosecution and my defence lawyer make their summings-up. The prosecuting lawyer is as damning as ever, accusing those who supported me of lies. When he finishes, the courtroom is again in an uproar and my defender Kirby has difficulty in making himself heard. However he repeats all that has been said of the help I gave to both Klara and the sergeant. It is next the judge's turn to speak, and he instructs the jury in his most serious voice, pointing out the gravity of the decision they must make. It is a question of who is to be believed, and even if I did show kindness to two individuals, it does not prove my innocence. His words sound as doom-laden as those of the prosecution.

The eight jurymen now go into a side room to consider their verdict. The court is adjourned, and under my escort, I am returned to the jailhouse and locked in my cell. For what seems forever I await the decision that will decide my fate. I have no doubt that a guilty verdict will result in a sentence of execution. I try to sleep, but am too restless, and the cold wind biting through my small window has me shivering. But suddenly recollections of Klara, of her lovely green eyes, fill my mind and I wish with all my heart that I could somehow rescue her from the grip of her awful husband.

At last keys rattle in the cell door and Marshal Frazer tells me that I am to return to the courthouse. Ten minutes later, I am again before Judge Smith. I watch as the jury returns and the judge asks their foreman for the verdict. The man pauses before passing the judge a note. The judge reads slowly, extracting every ounce of drama from the situation. As for me, my chest feels constricted. I can hardly breathe.

The judge now asks me to stand which I do despite my trembling legs. At last his words come.

'You have been judged not guilty of the charges against you. This leaves me no alternative but to give a pronouncement of acquittal. It is now my decision that you will be returned to the custody of the army so that you may be conveyed to Alcatraz to serve the life sentence which has already been served upon you. This time I am sure that the army will prevent any further opportunity for you to escape.'

I do not remember much of the remaining days I spend in the Yreka jail. All I know is that they are overshadowed by thoughts of what now awaits me. I wonder if the army will place me before a further tribunal on the charge of escaping.

I have no regrets as I quit Yreka. A troop of bluecoats, all heavily armed, come to collect me and soon I am being taken along the road past the upper Klamath Lake, secured in the back of an army wagon. My hands and ankles are chained. It is a cold but sunny day. I glance at the sky, at the surrounding forests, hear the birds, and once see a wolf watching us from the shadows of the trees. How I envy them their freedom!

My future seems to offer two alternatives:

either my death sentence will be restored; perhaps a special new scaffold will be erected for my benefit. Or on the other hand, I will recommence my interrupted journey to the dismal place called Alcatraz.

Once I arrive amid the familiar buildings of Fort Klamath – a sight I hoped never to see again – I am not kept in suspense for long. Soon I am standing before the commanding officer, Colonel Wheaton. He is the soldier-chief who read out the proclamation from President Grant, the proclamation that saved Slolux and me from hanging. Now he sits at his desk. He wastes no fancy words.

'As soon as possible,' he says, 'you will start out for Alcatraz. There, I promise you, your life sentence will be served. Not even pretending to be an idiot will do you any good. That is all I have to say.'

Ten minutes later I am back in the guard-house. This time I am the only prisoner in this cell where I spent so many miserable weeks. I never dreamed I would come back.

But matters do not move quickly. For

151

what seems weeks I languish in that cell at Fort Klamath, manacled most of the time. The army has no intention of losing me again and I am told that Slolux is already at Alcatraz, though he is still sick.

The regimental barber gets to work, ruthlessly hacking off my shoulder length locks. He even scrapes my face with a razor. I fear he is about to cut my throat; he does not, though he makes my skin raw. He shaves me smooth as a baby's arse. Afterwards, when I look in a mirror, I do not recognize myself. It seems I am no longer Barncho; I do not even look like a Modoc. But then I remember that, in truth, I am not a Modoc. I am a white man, though I am sure nobody guesses.

I am issued with new clothes – thick coat, woollen jersey, linen shirt, army pants and boots. The pants are far too large and have no belt. They will trip me if I try to run away. At least they would do, but I find some string and tie them up. Anyway, I am in chains so how can I run off?

On my final morning at Fort Klamath, I am once again placed in an enclosed wagon. Under escort I am conveyed along the Rancheria Road. I leave Fort Klamath with no regrets, only fear of the future.

My state of fear continues over the next days, for I am moving through a world that is completely strange to me. Still heavily manacled in meat-cleaver chain and leg irons, I am transferred to the cattle-car of a train. The iron-horse hisses, snorts forth smoke and cinders. My guards laugh as they see how nervous I am at the click-clacking wheels, the sway and roar, the way this monster unleashes its unworldly catawauling. My guards are bearded, hard-faced men who bark orders at me like enraged dogs and often kick me. They smoke cigarettes and swap jokes of which I only catch snatches but suspect they concern women's bodies. I long to hear again the Modoc tongue, but that is impossible. Through the long hours of this journey I am allowed little movement.

Freezing winter is now settling in. Three

days later we reach the great settlement that is San Francisco, where, I am told, countless persons live. It has grown out of man's greed for yellow iron and now has buildings taller than any I have ever seen. I am led from the train, hobbling in my ankle irons. We move along the platform, passing through steam spewed out from the iron-horse. We come clear of some buildings and snow touches our faces. One of the guards remarks that it has blown all the way from Alaska, though how he knows I cannot imagine.

It is now I get my first sight of the ocean. Nothing has prepared me for this, not even the expanses of my homeland lakes.

Standing upon the quayside, the place called Fisherman's Wharf, I gaze out at the restless swirl of angry white-capped waves. It stretches away into the murk of fog.

At the quayside, several people pause to gape at me, their eyes incredulous. In the brief glow of a match as a man lights his cigarette, I see an expression of absolute contempt. Maybe they have heard that I am a 'wild' Indian, utterly savage though now restrained like a shackled bear intended to entertain an audience. I glare at them, show my teeth in a snarl. I must not disappoint them.

A large barge with a funnel is moored at the quayside, pitching fiercely upon the wind-stirred swells. I allow myself to be forced from solid ground on to its heaving deck, fearing that if I tumble overboard my chains will quickly drag me to the black, icy depths. But I survive to reach the pilot-house, balancing desperately to keep my footing. The captain shouts out orders to his crew and the barge casts off from the shore. I wonder if I will ever return. Somewhere ahead in the fog, I know, is Alcatraz Island. For some strange reason I imagine that it will be as unstable as this barge.

Already my stomach is churning, queasiness rising to my throat, and a moment later as we strike out into the waves, my guts rebel and I throw up, much to the revulsion of my guards.

I am made to drop to my knees, to grovel in my own slime on the heaving floor as the journey across the bay proceeds. The barge seems to plunge through the waves rather than over them, keeping the deck and pilot-house windows constantly awash.

This mile we have to travel across the bay may just as well be a thousand for all my sickened mind knows. Even the storm-tossed lakes of Mawatoc never displayed such turmoil. The boards upon which I sprawl seem alive beneath me, rising and falling as if determined to shake my insides out. I vomit until my stomach is empty, longing for death to provide relief. It does not.

Eventually I lift my head and gaze out through the rainswept window.

Now, directly ahead, is the bleak hulk of Alcatraz Island. A brooding mass of rock rearing from the sea, its sides sloping pre-cipices. A building sits upon its mesa top; near it a flashing beacon pierces the gloom. I recall Sergeant Hardeman's words: *When you see Alcatraz, you will wish you had died with Jack and the others.*

The moment I have feared for so long, struggled so desperately to avoid, is almost upon me. But already one word is pounding in my head, though only God knows how I will make it more than an impossible dream.

Escape!

CHAPTER TWELVE

I lie on the boards, trying to keep a grip on my guts. I am aware that my guards are struggling to retain their feet, but even so are laughing at my predicament. Then I notice a change coming over them and their attention turns away from me. Suddenly a jolting shudder runs through the barge and the crew are shouting.

I panic. Have we struck a rock? Are we about to sink?

Then I realize that we have reached Alcatraz. I am dragged to my feet and through the window I see the wharf. Later I will learn that it is the only safe landing place on the island. Men are rushing around, appearing in and out of the fog as they fasten the barge to its moorings. Everything is bathed, on and off, in a red glow. It comes from the beacon on the summit. Later I will learn that this is to warn ships at sea of the dangerous rocks. Now, to me, it just adds to the nightmare. My ears are filled with screeching sounds and looking up I see that there are hundreds of gulls whirling in and out of the fog. Their wings seem huge.

Once again, I am pushed forward. The climb from the barge to the shore is perilous for the waves are angry and I again fear that I am going to fall and drown. But at last my feet are on the stones of the wharf, although, as I struggle to stand, they give the impression of instability.

I am unable to study my surroundings for the fog seems thicker than ever, but I am aware of sentries pacing stiffly up and down along parapets, rifles across their shoulders. Two soldiers seize my arms and I am forced up some steps, my chains clinking. We pass beneath twin arches, across a drawbridge and through some heavy oak doors, and I realize that we have entered a guardhouse. It is large, almost a fort in itself.

A thickset man is seated at a desk. There are three chevrons on the arm of his blue tunic. He looks up at me. He has a face like a frog. Above his head is a board proclaiming: *4th United States Artillery.*

'So this is the dreaded One-Eyed Modoc Kid,' he says. 'Welcome to Alcatraz. He don't look so "dreaded" now, just looks like the loony he is. And by the way, I hate Injuns. The Sioux killed my brother, tore the scalp from his head.'

I do not respond.

He signs the paper with a flourish, and says: 'Received one live body – if you can call him that!'

He hands the paper to the captain who touches the peak of his cap and says: 'Thank you, Sergeant Hush. Now I got to get back across that Bay. The weather is as crazy as this rock.' He turns and departs.

Sergeant Hush looks back towards me, is about to speak. It is then I find my voice. 'Is Slolux here?'

'Ah,' he replies. 'The creature has a

160

tongue! Slolux? Damn Injun! Had no brain. I guess he didn't like the accommodation. Coughed himself to death last week. They call it scrofula.' He smiles smugly as if his knowledge of the word gives him pleasure.

I sigh angrily, jerk uselessly at my chains.

'I'll tell you something else,' Sergeant Hush continues. 'Nobody, not a single soul, ever escapes from Alcatraz. And you will never be allowed to communicate with the outside world.'

He seems all at once to grow impatient; he has wasted enough time on me. He snaps out orders to the bluecoats holding me: 'Take him away, wash the filth from him, issue him his clothes, then toss him into the black hole. That'll show him what this place is like.' He dismisses me with a nod.

The guards hustle me from the sergeant's presence.

For a moment I am back again in the damp fog; then we pass through another heavily-studded door and I am in a large room with a beamed ceiling and brick floor.

One of the guards, a corporal, has been given keys and now he unfastens my chains, allowing them to fall to the ground, but I have little time to enjoy the relief.

'Strip off – everything!' the corporal orders and as I hesitate: 'Hurry up for God's sake!' and then their cruel hands tear the clothes from my body leaving me entirely naked. They stand back sniggering at my stumpy frame, grinning at my small dick. I am shuddering with the freezing cold, but worse is to follow. Soon, buckets of frigid salt water are being sloshed over me, drenching me from head to toe, cutting my breath. I stand rigidly still, determined to withstand this torture without crying out. If ever I attempt to swim to freedom I will have to get used to freezing water. Now it streams down over my head, face, shoulders and body for what seems an age and then a heap of dried clothing is thrown at me. It is a threadbare army uniform, stripped of brass buttons and trim, long cotton drawers and socks. I have never worn socks in my life. I see that there is a big white 'P' on the back of the uniform's blouse.

'Cover yourself up, Injun. You ain't no pretty sight, for sure.'

I am still dripping wet, but I am glad enough to cover my nakedness. It seems crazy; me wearing the uniform of a bluecoat. My boots are replaced by backless canvas moccasins. Still shivering I am led back into the cold, along a roadway, through a sally-port into the guardhouse. I do not see the sergeant again, but am forced towards an iron grill in the floor. This is dragged open and I see a ladder leading down into a dark hole. I am pushed onto the ladder and to avoid falling I set my feet on the rungs and grasp the sides.

'Get down there before we push you down!' the corporal cries.

I can do nothing but comply. As I descend into the gloom and step onto the floor below, I am aware that the ladder has been drawn up; then the grill is slammed back into place. I hear a chain rattling as it is padlocked.

Every sound seems echoey and three times louder than it should be. I find myself alone in this freezing hole – a fetid dungeon with black-painted walls. I touch them; they are dripping with moisture. There is no way I can climb up to the grating which admits faint light. The walls are smooth and twice as tall as me. Even if I could climb up, I would be unable to open the grating.

There is no pallet, no furnishings apart from a bucket. Will I remain here for the rest of my life, what is left of it? Always alone? All I can do is sit upon the floor, rest my back against the wall and attempt to find some warmth in the dampness of the clothes they have given me. I have started my life sentence in Alcatraz prison. I fear, like Slolux, I will die here.

I weep.

The light filtering down from the grating gradually melts into complete darkness. I feel as if I am in an ice house. Curled into a ball, I lay on the hard floor while the hours drag by. There is scurrying about me and I suspect that I have rats for company. Thoughts crisscross through my mind, a jumble of memories, regrets, sadness, fears, faces, wishes for relief ... and realisation of the impossibility of escape. I am without hope.

At long, long last, thin light begins to filter through the grating, and presently from above, in the distance, I hear the sound of a bugle. This must be reveille and I am reminded that I am in a military post, an army fort, just as Fort Klamath was. The fact that Fort Klamath is so far away, by rail, road and sea, deepens my misery. It seems that this white man's world, heavily populated, is vast beyond anything that Indian people can understand. White people are like an immense sea that is rapidly flowing into every space. What hope can there be for the Indian?

And then I suddenly remember. While I think like an Indian, suffer like an Indian, I was born a white man. I am an in between man, of value to nobody.

I am roused from my melancholy by the rattling of chains from above. The grating is being dragged open and glancing up, I see faces peering down at me.

'Wake up, Injun,' somebody calls. It is a guard whom I have not seen before. 'That's if you want breakfast!'

There is a scraping sound. The ladder is being lowered into my hole. I scramble to my feet. My legs feel like lead, my head aches, my mouth foul. Even so I climb upwards, and as I step out from the hole I find that I have two guards as companions. They are both holding heavy truncheons and I have no wish to be beaten so I comply quickly with their orders and walk in the direction indicated.

Ten minutes later I am in a hall. There are several long tables at which men are seated, heaping their tin plates with sausage, potatoes, bread rolls and helping themselves to coffee. There must be over fifty men, all dressed in old army uniforms. Glancing amongst them, I shudder. There is not one

Indian face here.

One of my guards tells me: 'All deserters, murderers, thieves, rapists. A lot of bad eggs in one basket.'

'All sojers?' I ask.

'Sure. Fifty hard case soldiers ... and you – one goddam Injun. Bit one-sided, eh?' He and his companion find the thought amusing for they both laugh. Then they indicate where I should sit. It is at a table with six others.

'That's your place in future,' I am told. 'Don't forget, otherwise you'll starve!' Then they walk off.

I have not realized how hungry I am. I tuck in to the food; at the same time I am aware of the glances that come in my direction, glances that tell me that 'Injuns sure ain't appreciated.' I wonder if any of these men took part in the Lava Beds War. Maybe I shot at some of them.

Gradually previous conversation resumes.

'Escape from this place can be done,' one man is saying.

'Only in dreams, Kelvin. It is a mile's swim to either San Francisco or Angel Island, the current'd most likely force you back here, that's if you didn't freeze to death in the water.'

'Or be swallowed by damned sharks?' another man cuts in. 'I hear the bay's swarming with them.'

But the first speaker, Kelvin, is not deterred. 'I still say it is possible. You'd have to get away after last roll call. That would give you about nine hours before they missed you.'

I would like to ask the question: 'How?' But I do not, and concentrate on munching the bread. It is stale but good.

When most of the prisoners are finished eating, the order is given to stand up and chairs scrape as men come to their feet. A moment later I take my place in line and we pass through a doorway and are counted. Some men are checked to ensure that they are not taking knives and forks with them. With armed guards watching us carefully, we are shortly within another large hall. This is for recreation. My company is unwanted and I am left standing alone while others mill around or stand talking. We remain in the exercise hall until eventually we are again called into line and counted. At this time I am surprised to be beckoned by a guard.

He leads me up some steps and I am outside again. This is when I get my first good look at Alcatraz Island and I am even more convinced that this is the most grim place in the world. It is a long, narrow island rearing from the sea like a half drowned mountain. It is dotted with buildings, some only half built. At its summit is a large three-storey barrack block. My guards direct me along one of many terraces, and we pass numerous embankments where huge iron guns stand, pointing out to sea. Behind these hundreds of cannon balls are stacked, and the sight of these reminds me of how we were bombarded while in the Stronghold, of how they exploded as we sheltered in the caves.

Glancing across the sea, I see the outline of San Francisco backed by hills. It looks far away. The thought of swimming through the icy water, fearing that at any moment a great fish will eat me, is daunting and for the moment I dismiss it from my mind. There must be other ways. Perhaps I can build a canoe.

Shortly we come to a low wooden building surrounded by a stockade wall, and on entering I see that it has about a dozen small cage-like cells lining each side. The place smells of men packed closely together. Faces gaze out through the iron bars.

In the centre gangway, an ancient looking stove is roaring. The top is off and sparks are shooting towards the ceiling while an orderly piles in logs.

From one of the cells a man shouts out: 'For God's sake be careful! If this place catches fire, it'll burn like dry tinder. We'll be roasted alive in these damned cages!'

The orderly carries on piling logs into the stove. 'Better than freezing to death,' he

170

calls back.

My allotted cell is at the far end. I am bundled into it, the door is slammed shut the key turned. This is my new home.

CHAPTER THIRTEEN

My cell is square with thick plastered walls on three sides, iron bars on the fourth. Its walls are about the length of a normal man, but being short I have room to spare. The only furnishings are a straw-filled pallet, a wooden chair, two shelves and a bucket. There is no blanket. I grip the bars, trying to find some looseness but they are as solid as rock. I can hear men calling to each other from the other cells, but I have no wish to join in. To them I am 'Injun scum' and therefore one to be hated. I groan with frustration, collapse onto my pallet, close my eyes. I adopt my old habit of retreating into myself, allowing memories to roam through my head. More and more often, dreams of Klara come, yet when I awake, the prospect of never seeing her again is torture. I wonder what anguish her man has since inflicted upon her. I try to place her in a part of my mind where she will be forever treasured, forever safe. Then I try to turn my thoughts to other days.

Suddenly I am free and in the open spaces of Mawatoc, beneath blue skies, breathing in air fresh from the mountains. I can hear my Indian companions laughing, the cries of children, the murmur of women and hear the calls of larks above me. For how long I enjoy this freedom, I have no way of telling. There are no clocks or overhead sun to indicate the passage of time. All I know is that presently a guard appears at my door and turns the key in the lock. He is carrying the usual thick truncheon.

'We got work for you to do, Barncho,' he says. 'You come with me.'

Some things I have already learned. Never argue with a guard. I follow him like a servile dog. I notice that most of the other cells are now empty, their doors open. A minute later I am outside again, my feet scraping along in the backless moccasins. The bite of the wind is sharp, but the day is surprisingly bright, the fog gone, the sun shining in a blue sky. Screaming gulls and cormorants swarm above our heads, rising from their nests in the cliffs, while along the roadway blue-uniformed guards pace monotonously. It seems that there are more guards than prisoners.

We climb up the steps through terraces, and I see again the great iron guns pointing out to sea, standing upon their platforms. Behind each is a neat stack of cannon balls. Many of these are shiny with fresh paint, as if their main purpose is for decoration. After climbing for some minutes, we reach a pyramid of unpainted cannon balls and I realize what my job is. Alongside stand several cans of paint and some brushes. How useless this task is! If these cannon balls are fired they will explode and all the paint-work will be wasted. Anybody on the receiving end will not care whether they are green or black.

The guard orders me to stand still, then drags from the side a heavy ball and chain. He locks the chain to my leg and I know that any movement which I will now make will be slow and cumbersome. But at least this is better than being locked in a cell.

We are high on the face of a cliff, standing on a granite platform.

Before starting work, I glance around again. The island is about a mile long and a half-mile wide – the shape of a great footprint set in San Francisco Bay. It's cliffs are lined with man-made terraces. At regular intervals along these stand the cannons, each mounted on a platform. For the first time I consider that the Americans have enemies other than Indians. Later I learn that threats on San Francisco from far off invaders have always been feared. Alcatraz stands as a formidable guard in addition to being a prison.

Even from this distance, I can see how the water is creased with swirling, treacherous currents. I wonder about the sharks cruising beneath. The Bay is cluttered with many boats of various sizes, some with sails. In the distance there are other islands, as well as the serrated coastline that is San Francisco.

Behind and above me upon the island's summit sits a large barrack block. It has three storeys. Later I learn that this is called 'The Citadel' and it is where the guards and their families live. It is surrounded by a ditch which can only be crossed at two draw-bridges, one at each end of the building. To one side is the lighthouse, the blink of its light continuing unceasingly. Glancing downward, I can see the wharf where I landed. The guardhouse and sallyport stand close to the water's edge. They straddle the hill leading inland. At the dockside a barge is moored. Perhaps it is the same one that carried me across. Barrels are being unloaded from it by men who look like ants from this distance. I learn later that the barrels contain water to supply the barren rock.

This entire island is a bastion. I am reminded of our stronghold in the lava beds.

What happened there, when we repelled the bluecoats, seems like a hundred years ago. Those were proud days, despite everything.

Plunging downward from the Citadel, are great precipices. Elsewhere I can see a drill square where some soldiers are marching back and forth. The shouted commands of their noncoms carry clearly on the wind. There are many long wooden buildings, sheds and storehouses. Amongst these, men are working, moving rocks, building walls, digging holes. The whole island is swarming with activity, and everywhere is coated with a layer of snow that glints in the sunshine.

I work steadily with the paintbrush and am aware that my guard is not paying me much attention. Other eyes are upon me, those of two small white children, a boy and girl, both blond, who, in realizing that I have spotted them, are overcome with peels of laughter. Is my appearance that strange? A woman's voice calls to them, and they scamper up the roadway. Their mother is standing, her red dress billowing in the breeze, her hair blond like that of her children. It is not only prisoners and guards who live on this island, but families as well. As I continue painting, the sun moves across the sky.

I am on my third can of paint, when a bugle sounds and there is a mass movement towards the dining hall. The guard comes and unfastens my ball and chain. Later, as I eat, I listen to the talk going on about me. It is always about escape from Alcatraz.

The following days stretch into monotonous routine of being fed, working hampered by a ball and chain in many, various tasks often in freezing, foggy weather, often for twelve hours each day. We are at last granted a luxury. Each prisoner is issued with two blankets.

There are of course periods in the recreation hall and some of the prisoners even pass the odd word with me. Although reluctant at first, they gradually accept me.

The days are punctuated by military routine: the unending succession of bugle calls and drum rolls which mark the passage of time. Soldiers carry out a variety of daily exercises, alternating between marching drills, artillery practice, maintenance work, dress parades and sundry inspections. In addition there is frequent cannon-firing practice.

We are forever being counted, in and out of our cells – and always at nightfall we are confined in those cages, keys are turned and we are trapped until somebody lets us out. What heat there is comes from the stove in the centre gangway but it is little enough.

At reveille another day of work commences with the inevitable bugle call. We are stripped twice a week, and freezing water is pumped onto our bodies as we line up, but now I withstand with fortitude what was once torture. Sometimes at night I dream I am swimming in the sea, gradually getting nearer to the shore and freedom. At meal and recreation times I keep my ears open, listening for any hint as to how an escape could be achieved, but nobody ever seems to suggest anything that is feasible.

But now my pattern of work is changing. I am gradually establishing a pattern of trust and I am no longer hampered by a ball and chain, but allowed to work at the great variety of tasks, digging, painting, building, unloading items from the barge and even carrying errands for the guards. I feel I am losing my Indian identity, becoming more like the white man I am. It seems that any consideration of getting away from the island is not considered feasible by the authorities. The shark-infested, ice cold sea, the dangerous currents, the constant watchfulness of guards all combine to discourage such consideration.

Yet freedom beckons me. I still watch for my chance.

Gradually winter gives way to spring. As the weeks pass the sun shines more frequently, the sea reflects the blueness of the sky. Snow concedes to scrubby patches of grass, gull-chicks appear in the cliff nests and pouch-beaked pelicans strut the island, their screeching vying with the wind's bluster.

One night the ancient stove in the centre of our gangway explodes, sending flames shooting up into the rafters of the old prison block. Men are awakened by the fierce crackle of tinder-dry timbers catching alight and terror of being burned alive, trapped in their tiny cells, spreads panic. The heat about us intensifies and as smoke grows dense, men's cries and coughing rise above the roar of flames and there seems no sign of the guards. It appears they are slumbering in their end-room undisturbed, but with the heat becoming suffocating their alarmed shouting at last sounds. Then comes the rattle of keys as a mad rush is made to unlock the cells. Inmates tumble out, gasping for air, scrambling madly for the end door, me included.

We all group outside, standing around as soldiers, in various stages of night attire, hurriedly bring water to douse the flames. It takes a good hour before the fire is extinguished. Next day and with great reluctance prisoners return to their cells, the air still tainted by the blackened timbers.

Two days later a new stove is installed, but fear of being burned alive lingers with us.

In July three prisoners attempt to disprove the belief that Alcatraz is escape-proof. After breaking clear, they remain hidden in caves on the north side of the island, before they are eventually discovered. As they attempt to run off, the guards unleash a hail of bullets, killing all three. It is a grim reminder of the dangers in trying to get away from Alcatraz. But it somehow makes my own determination even stronger.

The nights spent in my tiny cage seem endless, for I do not sleep easily, each crackle from the stove disturbing me. My days are a tedious grind – and the great grandfather in Washington has ordered that I am to remain here for life. A living death.

Yet for others this island is not a purgatory. Sometimes families come down from their home in the Citadel, the women in their bright dresses and carrying parasols. They take walks along the roadways, exploring the island, standing to watch prisoners at work. Sight of them is not unwelcome for they make a change from the drabness of all-male company. It must be a very strange life for them here. Apart from the real hard-cases who are kept locked away, most of the prisoners are allowed to wander freely and there is very little trouble. They sometimes chat with the families. There are far more children than I imagined and frequently they run about the roadways and terraces. I even play hopscotch with the two blond children. The boy's name is Charlie, the girl's Ellie. They tell me that that their father is the commanding officer of Alcatraz, Major Morgan.

One popular pastime which creates great cries of joy among the children, is riding in small wheeled carts. They have canvas sheets for sails. They whiz along the roadways at incredible speed, sometimes causing prisoners and guards to leap out the way. I notice that the Morgan children ride in a bread-kneading trough, no doubt discarded by the bakery. They call me Good Old Barncho, though they do not know that what is in my head is not often good.

There is no point in being disobedient or lazy. I have always been industrious by nature and this seems to be noticed. As summer lengthens, I am given increasing freedom, often carrying messages to different parts of the island. I become known to the guards, perhaps viewed as a harmless, simple-minded native. But inwardly I remain vigilant, my senses alert. If escape from this island offers itself in any form, I will either succeed in gaining freedom or die in the attempt. I await my chance, ever watchful.

I explore the island, wandering the terraces, studying the great guns and the soldiers as they train on them. It seems I become an accepted part of the scenery for little notice is taken of me. Sometimes I wander along the narrow rocky shoreline, exploring caves. But I am careful never to give the impression of taking advantage of my freedom, limiting the periods I take in my wanderings, delivering my messages promptly and ensuring that I am always back for the inevitable counting and nightly lock-up. Many of the other prisoners, all soldiers, complete their spells on the island, some of them returning to duty, others, who have offended more seriously, being dismissed from the army. But for me, release is not a consideration. President Grant has said 'for life'.

Fall, then winter return. The island again becomes blanketed in almost constant fog. The dismal hoot of ships' horns from the Bay, the cries of birds, the shouts of the guards, the clink of pick-axes biting into rock, the grumblings of my companions, the rattle of keys in locks, all form the dreary backdrop to my days. But still I find sunshine in the memory of Klara's smile and green eyes. I wonder how little Agata is and if her mother sometimes tells her of 'the angel who saved her at birth'.

I am now moving into my second year on Alcatraz. Despite giving the impression of docility, I remain alert.

And one day when the brightness of another summer comes to the island dispelling its foggy gloom, my watchfulness is rewarded. A slim chance offers itself to me, coming from a completely unexpected source.

CHAPTER FOURTEEN

It happens in the strangest of ways. For once my mind is not on escape. I am alone and working at the platform of a gun emplacement. I am concentrating on the tedious process of scraping mortar from old bricks in readiness for their future use. This July morning is already hot and the sun is a brassy ball in the sky. My mind has drifted to far off Oklahoma where my people have been sent. I have heard nothing from them for over three years. I wonder how my Modoc mother and father are, even if they are still alive and if they sometimes remember the white boy they reared as their own.

As I so often am, I am working on the southern face of a cliff. Behind me the roadway zigzags downward before levelling out to a flatter patch. Suddenly I hear children screaming and turning, I see a little trolley careering downhill at out of control speed, its sail speeding its headlong descent. I catch a glimpse of blond hair and realize that it is the Morgan children and they are in desperate trouble. This is no longer a game for the wall is low at this point and the trolley, the old bread-kneading trough, is no longer an item for play, but a death trap.

The children are kneeling within it, both screaming, the girl clinging to the boy's back. Suddenly she loses her grip and as the trolley races around the curve, she is catapulted clear. But no such fortune for the boy.

A second later the trolley is plunging through the low parapet, jumping upward as it strikes a small boulder.

I am on my feet instantly, rushing towards the point where it disappeared. I know below there is a further terrace, and then a drop onto rocks. Conscious of the girl's groans of pain, I run to the gap in the parapet and gaze down. The trolley lies like a discarded toy on the terrace below. I glance desperately around for sight of the boy. He seems to have disappeared. Then suddenly I spot him. He is sprawled motionless some fifteen feet down. He could have rolled further and plunged downward to where the water crashes in white plumes against the rocks. I glance around for help but see nobody.

Quickly I scramble across the parapet, lower myself downward. The going is dangerous and steep. One slip and it could be the end of me, but somehow I reach the boy and crouch over him. Amazingly he is still alive but he has struck his head and he is covered in blood. I gather him in my arms and begin the perilous climb back. Moments later I have reached the platform, young Charlie still in my arms. The girl is scrambling to her feet, white faced and shaken.

'Is he…?'

'He'll probably be all right,' I say, though I'm far from sure. Indeed as I hold him, striving to regain my breath, I fear that already I am too late – but then he groans and I sigh with relief.

Still holding him, I climb to the roadway and round the curve. Above me on the summit I can see the Citadel. This is where Charlie and his sister live. I must get him there as quickly as I can. He will need a doctor. His head has a terrible gash in it and his eyes remain closed but his breathing continues steadily. It takes me ten minutes to reach the drawbridge of the Citadel, the girl rushing along behind. I have never entered this place before. The sentry standing at the gateway realizes the gravity of the situation and waves me onward.

'Through the main door … at the end of the corridor!'

As I enter the place Mrs Morgan rushes into view, an anguished cry on her lips. She takes her son from me, carrying him through into another room. She calls out: 'Get the doctor – quick!' and a servant girl dashes past me and disappears down the corridor. The little girl Ellie, her face red with bruises, gives me a desperate glance and then follows after her mother.

For a moment I am left standing alone. It seems I have been forgotten. I'm still covered in the boy's blood. Shortly I hear the rush of feet and the rotund red-faced doctor comes hurrying along the corridor, a leather bag in his hand. He enters the room where the boy has been taken. Within a moment I can hear anxious voices from within.

I turn, walk back along the way I have come. As I pass the sentry he asks: 'Is the boy okay!'

I shake my head. 'I don't know.'

I reach the roadway, reach the spot where I was working when the accident occurred. I glance over the parapet edge and see the trolley lying on the terrace below – a large cooking utensil, strong enough to withstand the heat of an oven, strong enough to remain undamaged after a fifteen foot drop, apart from smashing its wheels. Its canvas sail is now caught in the wind, flapping like a flag.

It seems unnecessary to continue working.

It is nearly time for the midday meal. I decide to walk to the dining hall, but as I start off my eye again catches the trolley lying on the terrace below. As if drawn by some instinct, I clamber down towards it, my progress now less frantic. I see its tin is undented. It is big enough to take two children. One small man would easily fit in it. Even the wooden mast, still with its canvas sail, is not broken.

As I stand looking at it an odd feeling comes over me. I see the narrow rocky shore beneath the lowered terrace and how it is backed by the shallow cave. I have explored it previously. Now the first germ of an idea grows in me. I grasp the trolley, and reaching down to my full extent, I allow it to drop to the rocks below. I immediately follow it down, drag it into the cave. I am thankful that it has no holes in it. I am trembling with excitement and yet the idea forming in my mind is of the most vague nature.

Later, I eat my food barely conscious of the conversation going on around me. My head is swirling with possibilities.

In the early afternoon, an orderly comes to me as I work at the bricks. 'The commanding officer wants to see you, Barncho. Better get your arse up to the Citadel quick! He don't like being kept waiting.'

Ten minutes later I am standing in front of this man who rules over Alcatraz. He looks tremendously pompous in his uniform which has gold braid upon it. He is very stout. But for a fringe of curly, nearly white hair at the back of his head, he is quite bald. He appears much older than his wife. He sits behind his desk, his face red and with a network of purple veins on his cheeks.

He rises to his feet and to my surprise extends his hand which I shake. 'We owe you a great debt of gratitude,' he says. 'You undoubtedly saved my son's life. I cannot thank you enough.'

He walks around his desk, his face beaming with relief. 'The doctor says he had an amazing escape, had he fallen a few more feet he would have fallen onto the rocks. As it is, he has a badly cut head and we are getting him to the mainland as quickly as possible. All I can say is that I shall never forget what you did. I shall issue orders that your life is to be made as easy as possible under the circumstances. Take the rest of the afternoon off. By golly, you've earned it.'

I try to speak but cannot. I have never been in such a situation before. In fact I have never spoken to the commanding officer previously. All I can do is nod in embarrassment. Before I leave he shakes my hand again. I thank God that he does not know what thoughts are going through my mind, what plans I'm making. Hopefully, when he does find out, it will be too late.

For the rest of the afternoon, I do not return to the cave where the trolley is hidden, but with every passing second the plan is growing firmer in my mind.

I take Major Morgan at his word. I am tired of scraping bricks. Apparently the major has passed word of his decision and when I tell an orderly that I'm not feeling well, he raises no objection to me returning to my cell. I find the place empty, the cell doors standing open. Everybody else is out at work. I too have work to do, but of a very different sort.

A few logs are piled near the stove. It is not alight for it is a hot day. I select two logs and carry them back to my cell and conceal them beneath my blanket. I then settle for a rest. I will need all my strength come later.

The man in the next cell to mine is called Bradley. He has never shown any resentment against Indians. When he returns to his cell, he listens in amazement as I tell him I am going to attempt to escape. He shakes his head in bewilderment but does not try to dissuade me.

'I am going to put the logs under the blanket, pile the second one underneath as well to make it look as if I am asleep on the pallet. When they come round to do the count, could you please say that I have been unwell and have slept most of the afternoon.'

I tell him of the day's events, and how I'm going to attempt to get away in the trolley. 'It's the warmest time of the year, the wind is blowing towards the shore and I think I have a good chance of making it.'

'Barncho,' he says, 'I shall say a prayer for you. You can have my blankets too. They will make it look even more as if you are in the pallet.'

I reach out and touch his shoulder. Not all white men, not all soldiers, are wicked, despite the sins they may have committed.

I cannot risk going to the eating hall this night although my stomach is rumbling. I take a long drink of water from the barrel at the end of the cell block. Every second is important to me now. For those who've seen me resting in my cell, the belief that I am unwell will ring true.

While the other prisoners are at their evening feed, I arrange my pallet to look as if it is occupied, the blanket drawn up over the log to look like my head. The block is deserted as I creep out. Nobody seems to take any notice of me. I drift inconspicuously to where I worked earlier in the day, clamber over the terraces and down the cliff. Expectation has me trembling. I am soon hidden in the cave's shadowy depths, satisfying myself that the trolley is seaworthy and the mast and sail will serve their purpose. The trough was once used for baking large quantities of dough in hot ovens, so it is sturdy. There is little left of the wheels and undercarriage which some indulgent carpenter had fixed with wire. What there is I pull clear. The mast and canvas sail are tiny. I am confident they will serve their purpose without capsizing the craft. In truth, it is simply a tin tub, but with the greatest fortune it will stay afloat and carry me far away. Perhaps such is the confidence of a fool. Within a few hours I may be drowned, but it is a chance I am determined to take.

This summer night, the light seems to take forever to fade from the sky, but the sea at this season is at its most calm. I hope that the currents swirling beneath the surface will be equally kind.

I rest on the hard rock floor of the cave, but I am too tense, too excited, to relax for long and my stomach is churning. As darkness eventually creeps in, the only sound I hear is the steady pound of ocean waves and the cries of birds. I wonder if my ruse has hoodwinked the guard into believing that I'm asleep beneath the blankets. I am sure Dave Bradley will have done his best. And if I am missed, at first they will not know where to look for me. If my dummy has passed the last count of the day, my cell locked, I will have some nine hours before my absence is discovered. By then I may be across the bay, or alternatively I may have been ripped to bloody bits by a shark.

When it is completely dark, I drag the trough out from the cave, across the shingle and launch it into the lapping waves. It almost capsizes as I scramble into it, but somehow I cope. My weight has it sinking deeper into the water but it is surprisingly buoyant, and using my cupped hands I start to bail out, then again using my hands I propel myself into deeper water and away from the shore. I am glad I am not a heavy man. The waves are stronger than I had anticipated, the sea more powerful, yet I know now that I must fight it. It is just over a mile across the bay to the shore. I am in the flimsiest of craft and I must not under-estimate the danger of the current. But hope is surging inside me.

As I get further from the shore, the trough is tossed this way and that, but the sail is catching the wind and I no longer use my hands as paddles. I am glad of this for I imagine the sharp teeth of sharks snapping not far beneath the surface. What better than a tasty hand for supper! In what seems an immense distance, I can see the lights of San Francisco twinkling.

That morning I had not dreamed that come nightfall I would be out upon the cold waters of San Francisco Bay, escape loom-ing before me like a beckoning finger. Any prospects I now have are hidden in the mysterious future.

As I progress, I am aware that the wind is growing stronger, the sea rougher. But still the blinking beacon of the lighthouse is behind me and growing more distant.

CHAPTER FIFTEEN

It is as if I am in a tiny tin coffin. There is not enough room to lie down and I sit crouched forward, my chin on my knees. I am aware of the incredible strength of the sea, the effects of the wind far greater than felt on land. Small waves lap against me, but amongst them larger rogue waves sneak up. My tiny vessel is very sensitive and yet somehow it keeps upright, bobbing like a cork. The wind has caught my sail, causing it to make a strange wailing sound. It is drawing me further away from the island, moving over the swells and dips at what seems incredible speed.

Just a mile, I think, just a mile to the mainland. Distance that as a boy I would have run in a few minutes yet here at sea everything is different because I am out of my element and reminded of my insignificance.

Behind, the red blink of the lighthouse beacon is growing even more distant. I glance around for the lights of other craft, but the waves form an undulating wall obscuring my view. Not that I want to encounter other boats.

I have no real control to direct myself. I am at the mercy of wind and current. The sea makes weird slapping sounds against the tin side of my craft. I do not even know if I'm heading towards the mainland. Perhaps somehow I have gone around the island and am sailing towards the far nothingness of what lies beyond – perhaps towards the edge of the world. But if not, sooner or later, I must strike land if I am not capsized before.

The sea consists of charging white horses that dash towards me in a welter of tumbling water. I feel as if I am some creature in a cocoon, a cocoon that may suddenly burst open. Waves drive into me, lifting my craft into the air as they roll then ease down, rushing on, slipping into the far shadow of distance.

I recall the sea as it had been during the day, sparkling. Now it is black and hostile, flecked with angry froth.

I close my eye and clench my teeth. Salt water is constantly splashing into my face. It leaves my throat parched. If only I could have brought some water or food, but I had no time and any unusual activity would have aroused suspicion. Just a mile, I keep telling myself, just a mile to the shore.

My body is shaking with cold, my one good eye stinging with salt. But my mind is filled with only one thing and that is the new desire for survival. The sea is growing ever rougher. To it, I am flotsam; it will offer me no mercy.

Above, the moon casts an intermittent silver glow across the scudding clouds. I strain my eye into the distance each time I am carried to the crest of a wave, longing for some indication of light that will mean San Francisco is ahead. I wonder what will happen to me when I land. I will hardly be welcomed with open arms. I will have to come ashore at a point when nobody is about, and slink off into shadows. How long will it be before word of my escape spreads? I will have to get away from the town as quickly as possible. Where will I go? It does not seem to matter as long as I have freedom.

Perhaps ultimately I will find my way to the Quawpaw Agency in Oklahoma and the reservation where the Modoc tribe has been located.

But that is a long way off and the prospects of crossing so many miles is daunting. The future must take care of itself. For the present all that matters is that I stay afloat and reach the shore.

This whirl of the current is turning me about. Could I be driven round in some sort of whirlpool which will ultimately suck me into its depths? Then everything will be over. What Barncho thinks or feels will no longer matter. The sea will fold me into its blanket.

A sudden new intensity of the sea scares

me. Glancing around I see that on each side, waves rise in vertical precipices and then plunge downward like watery avalanches. And now there is a new sound; it grows louder and louder like a herd of onrushing buffalo.

And then suddenly the very worst happens.

A huge escarpment of black sea looms out of the night, towering above me. It plunges downward, slams into me, overwhelms me, throws me from the tiny craft, crushing the air from my lungs.

I am sinking into a black oblivion that can only be the gateway to death. All hope is gone from me and I submit.

I roll in the surf. My knee scrapes against something solid, my mind grapples with what has happened. Surely I am dead, perhaps even now consumed by some monstrous fish of the depths. But no. I allow the tide to take hold of me, drawing me into shallower water. Again I feel my body scrape against something solid. I open my eye, see nothing; everything is blurred. I drag myself onward, somehow find the strength to pull my body clear of the lapping waves. I attempt to rise, but there is weakness in my legs, and all at once my stomach erupts, I am overcome by a bout of coughing and I spew up a volume of bile and seawater. I feel wretched. I collapse on soft sand. I am exhausted.

I realise that it is no longer dark. A desperate surge of energy seizes hold of me. Like some poor turtle dragging itself ashore, I haul myself higher onto dry ground. I rub my eye with my hand, at last restoring the vision. I envy men who have two eyes. For one awful moment the fear is in me that I have been washed back on to Alcatraz, but then glancing round I see giant oak trees. Some of these have been chopped down. Behind them green hills rise and the ground is lush with grass. Relief cuts through me. Alcatraz boasted no such vegetation – but this is not San Francisco either. Perhaps fortune has favoured me. Perhaps I have come ashore some miles along the coast, somewhere less populated where I can find concealment.

I'm starving and parched. Yet above all I am exhausted. I need somewhere to hide. I stagger onto my feet. The sun is rising. A new day is coming. Perhaps also, for me, a new birth. I drag myself to a clump of sage and coyote brush. My body aches and is sore in every part. I am trembling with cold but gradually the sun warms me. Reaching cover, I collapse, a great joy in my mind. I have escaped from the living death that is Alcatraz.

I do not know how long I sleep for; it may have been minutes or hours. It is not unusual, but somehow Klara finds her way into my dreams and I hug her, determined never to leave go, but as usual awakening snatches her away. As my senses absorb my situation, I can see that the sun is beginning its descent. Through the trees the sea shows. It picks its way among shoals and swampy islets with purpose and direction and I wonder how I ever found the strength or fortune to survive it.

Suddenly I am startled by a dreadful noise. I see the branches to my left swaying like frightened creatures. I cower down, wishing for a hole in the ground into which I could vanish. It is then that an old grey boar rushes through the undergrowth, unleashes a high-pitched squealing sound, then disappears into the trees. I force myself to be calm, but one concern persists. Something must have startled the beast.

By now my absence will have been discovered, but surely it will take quite a while for anybody to work out the means by which I got away.

When darkness comes I must make a move. Darkness must be my ally. The greater distance I can put between me and Alcatraz, the better my chances will be. My first priority will be to find food and water. The country around me seems well wooded and I believe that good fortune has brought me to the coastline somewhere north of San Francisco.

With a feeling of elation I climb to my feet.

I do not have a single possession in the world except for the damp prison clothing that I am wearing, but that is the least of my worries. I must wait until it is completely dark, then start my trek. With luck I will find a stream or perhaps an isolated farmhouse from which I can get some food – a theft, hopefully, that will go unnoticed. I have little chance of getting willing help from any other human, but I have been in such positions before and survived.

But as dusk creeps in all my hopes come crashing down.

Suddenly I hear movement close at hand and I freeze with alarm. Without further warning a soldier bursts through the trees, a rifle in his hands. More soldiers are crowding in behind him.

'What have we here?' he exclaims. For some crazy reason I notice he has huge black eyebrows.

Another man says: 'I think his shabby uniform gives him away. He's come from

Alcatraz all right.'

Somebody else chips in: 'Well, I guess it's a question of saying welcome to Angel Island, though God knows how he got across from Alcatraz.'

'One thing we can promise him and that is a one-way ticket back to where he came from.'

This brings a ripple of laughter from them.

A crazy urge is in me to make a run for it, but it is as if they sense my intensions. Their guns are immediately raised and I know I would not get more than a few yards before being riddled with bullets. I am gutted with disillusionment. All fight seems to leave me. I just collapse to the ground, pounding the earth with my fists, hearing their laughter ringing in my ears.

All my efforts have been in vain. It is not the San Francisco coastline that I landed upon, but Angel Island garrisoned by soldiers. I could have circled round, returned to Alcatraz, for all the good it has done me.

After a night in an army cell on Angel

Island, I am returned by barge to Alcatraz. I am handcuffed to an escort. The voyage seems to take only a few minutes. This seems crazy after the hours I spent in my little tin tub fighting the waves and currents and reaching what I firmly believed to be safety. My one good eye may be shedding tears. If it is, I wipe them away with the cuff of the coat I have been given.

It is pointless to recount the misery I feel when I am once again back in my old cell. But I am not given long to mope. This time I am allotted two orderlies who are completely silent as they escort me to the Citadel. I am kept standing for maybe ten minutes, then I am ushered into the presence of Major Morgan. This time his attitude is completely different from that of my previous visit. For a while he continues to write at some report, but eventually he deigns to look up and meet my eye. His expression is blacker than a thunder cloud. He throws his pen down upon his desk with a show of frustration.

'I thought I could trust you, Barncho,' he says. 'How foolish I was to disbelieve those who told me that no Indians could ever be trusted, that they were no better than rattlesnakes. I thought you were different. I was wrong. You have violated the trust I placed in you and you must be punished, punished in the most severest of ways.'

I can no longer meet his eye. I gaze at my feet. Perhaps I should offer him some plea of mercy, remind him of the last time we met, but I do not.

He says: 'I am sentencing you to nineteen days solitary confinement in the black hole. You will live on bread and water. Maybe I should have you flogged. That may come later.'

I am breathing heavily; thought of returning to the black hole is something that every man on Alcatraz fears. A sudden anger overtakes me. I draw myself up, glare at him.

'I am Modoc,' I say. 'I am not a bird to be trapped in a cage. And I did not kill General Canby.'

My words make no impression. He snaps out: 'Hold your tongue. *Dismiss!*'

As I am dragged towards the door a thought occurs to me. 'The boy ... is he all right?'

I dig my heels in, brace my legs, force my guards to pause for a moment. At first Major Morgan does not answer. It seems he is going to ignore me.

Then he shouts: 'Get him out of here!'

It is as my guards force me towards the door once again that his voice comes quite softly: 'The boy will recover.'

Within twenty minutes I am in the gloom of what seems like the bowels of the earth, the iron grating padlocked into place some eight feet above me; the black walls sur-rounding me dripping with moisture.

I doubt I will ever have the chance to escape from this island of Purgatory again. Why couldn't I have died with Jack and the others?

CHAPTER SIXTEEN

I exist in the black hole. It might surely be the same as being trapped in the belly of a mighty fish. I lose all idea of time; days and nights merge into gloomy nothingness and there is such little light that it gives me no indication. An hour could be a year before all I know. I have no hope. Even if I do emerge from this terrible place with some sanity, the future only offers more Purgatory. I cannot expect any more mercy or compassion from Major Morgan, and his sentiments will spread downward through his men. In his mind, I have betrayed him and that is something he will never forgive.

Chunks of stale bread and water, are lowered down through the grating in a bucket and the empty container lifted on the same rope. My sanitary bucket is emptied and replaced by the same means. The guards are forbidden to exchange even the briefest of words with me and the only relief I receive is when I am allowed out for lonely exercise once each day. For hours I sit with my back against the solid, moist wall, steeped in perpetual misery and trapped in what seems a void of time. I know that if I do emerge from this place, all freedom and privileges will have been withdrawn. My chains will always be with me.

All I can do is exist in my dank, gloomy prison, allow time to flow over me, and my brain to wander amid the gloomiest of thoughts. Even the images of Klara that drift into my head bring sadness, for I will never see her again. In these depths, little sound penetrates from above. I do not even hear the routine sounds of military activity. My only companions are rats, and I find little comradeship in them. Death will be welcome, but I am denied even the most primitive weapon with which I can inflict it. How wonderful it must be, to die on the battlefield, hurling oneself in glorious assault upon the enemy. But I have not even been granted a quick death at the end of a rope, nor the merciful end offered in the depths of the sea.

But at last my time comes. One morning the grating is opened and I am addressed by one of the guards for the first time in days. 'Barncho, it is time for you to come out of this stinking hole. You must go back to your cell!'

From now on I am not offered the privilege of work. I am kept under lock and key night and day, only being allowed the briefest of time in the exercise hall when other prisoners are elsewhere. I no longer eat in the dining hall, but my simple fare is brought grudgingly to my cell ... 'room service' as my jailers scornfully call it.

Then on the third day of my release from the black hole, an orderly comes to my cell and speaks words I never expected to hear again.

'Major Morgan wants to see you. Move your arse, Barncho!'

I cannot imagine the purpose of his summons. I suspect some further terrible punishment awaits me, perhaps the flogging. Hobbling along under the handicap of my chains, I follow the orderly up through the terraces and we cross the drawbridge and I feel strangely overawed, fearful as I am led along the corridor to the door that is marked 'Commanding Officer'.

This time there is no delay. Major Morgan is in his usual position behind his desk, his back to the window. But today he has company.

Seated opposite him is a black suited man in a strange frilled collar. He sits with his large black hat on his lap.

Barncho,' Major Morgan commences. 'I do not believe you deserve it, but you have been honoured by a visit from the most gracious gentleman. His name is Mr Jonathan Williams and he is from the Society of Quakers.'

I glance at this man. I feel wretched. My weeks in the black hole on the most meagre diet, restricted to the misery of solitary confinement, have left me little more than a gaunt skeleton.

In my weakened state, I am shown the first compassion I have received for many days. Mr Williams says, 'Sit down, Barncho. Otherwise you look as if you might fall down.'

My guard prods me towards a leather chair and I carefully lower myself into it. How strange it feels to enjoy the luxury of such a chair.

This Quaker man starts to speak. It is almost as if he has prepared a speech. 'The Society of Quakers, the Friends, has done great work in Africa. We have exposed that slavery still exists and it is being stopped. We feel the natives of this country deserve similar consideration. There is a new grandfather in Washington, President Hayes, and he is greatly concerned about the welfare of the Indians, particularly those in confinement. We Quakers have obtained thousands of signatures on a petition. There are many white people who deeply regret the treatment of the Indian population. We have encouraged President Hayes in the belief that every Indian, provided he acts like a civilised person, deserves the freedom of the reservation. The president has considered each case, one of which is yours.'

Mr Williams draws himself up in his chair, takes a deep breath. He holds up in his hand an important looking document. 'This is a declaration signed personally by the president. It says that you are to be released and sent to the reservation at the Quapaw Agency where the Modocs are living in Oklahoma. Provided you keep the peace and act in a responsible and civilised manner, you may remain there with your people.'

For a moment my mind is unable to absorb what is being said. It is beyond any dream. I glance at Major Morgan, expecting to see a frown of disapproval, but to my surprise he nods agreeably.

He looks at my guard. 'Unlock his chains,' he says. 'He can be released, conveyed to Oklahoma just as soon as the paperwork is completed.'

Three weeks later I am at the Quawpaw Agency in Oklahoma, as free as any Indian can be on reservation. Conditions are not good, but compared to Alcatraz it is like heaven. I enjoy a wonderful reunion with my mother. Sadly my father had passed into the spirit world. I cannot express the joy I experience at the return to these people. The fact that I was born a white man is no longer of relevance. I feel a Modoc through and through, and am proud of it.

And yet my story is not finished.

One day the greatest miracle happens. In the company of her sister and brother-in-law, a white woman arrives at the agency and asks to see the man called Michael Barncho. At first I feel I am dreaming just as I have so many times before, but she greets me with the happiest of laughs. Our hug is not one of kisses or passion. It is one that I hope will never relent. It is the Indian way. And I cannot speak because my heart beats, taking away my breath, overwhelming my every emotion.

But at last she draws back, her green eyes gazing into mine.

'Michael,' she is saying, 'thank God they set you free. You not deserve that punishment. I never forget what you did for me, how you appeared like an angel out of nowhere and helped my little girl into the world. I have told her the story so often and I have prayed for you every day since. Now, my prayers have been answered.'

Klara has blossomed with maturity, and now she is here, having crossed half a continent to find me.

'Ed my brother-in-law,' she says, 'has spoken to the authorities and they have given permission, if you want, for you to leave this agency and come to Oregon with us. We run a small farm, but we need a man to help us. Will you come?'

'Your husband?' I say. 'Where is he?'

She gives a resigned shrug. 'With the reward money he got for your capture, he went on an almighty binge. Got himself drunk, then fell out of his wagon, spent the freezing night lying on the trail. By morning he was dead.'

I nod. I will shed no tears for him.

'Michael,' she persists. 'Will you come to live on our farm? Help us with the work? It will not be too hard, I promise. Or do you need a little while to think about it?'

I look at her. I see again her green eyes, her beauty, and now there is a new radiance about her that even my dreams never captured. For a moment it seems I can see the soul that lies behind what she has suffered.

'I don't need time to think,' I say. 'I will come with you.'

This Large Print Book, for people
who cannot read normal print,
is published under the auspices of
THE ULVERSCROFT FOUNDATION

... we hope you have enjoyed this book.
Please think for a moment about those
who have worse eyesight than you ...
and are unable to even read or enjoy
Large Print without great difficulty.

You can help them by sending a
donation, large or small, to:

**The Ulverscroft Foundation,
1, The Green, Bradgate Road,
Anstey, Leicestershire, LE7 7FU,
England.**
or request a copy of our brochure for
more details.

The Foundation will use all donations
to assist those people who are visually
impaired and need special attention
with medical research, diagnosis
and treatment.

Thank you very much for your help.